The Fixers

Level Up
Book 2

JJ Anders

GRAYTON

Level Up ~ Pipers

DIGITAL ISBN: 978-1-945100-82-6

PHYSICAL ISBN:

Published by Grayton Press

Summary

Zane Noman had graduated from his level one lessons. This was a huge feat for a fatherless boy trapped within the confines of ECHO, the Ecological Colonies Habitat Organization, which kept him and several thousand others alive on an uninhabitable planet called Amara.

Now that his first level classes are completed, he returns to his home hub, the Pipes, for his break. He once again finds himself having adventures and hiding from dangers that will haunt him throughout his second year of training.

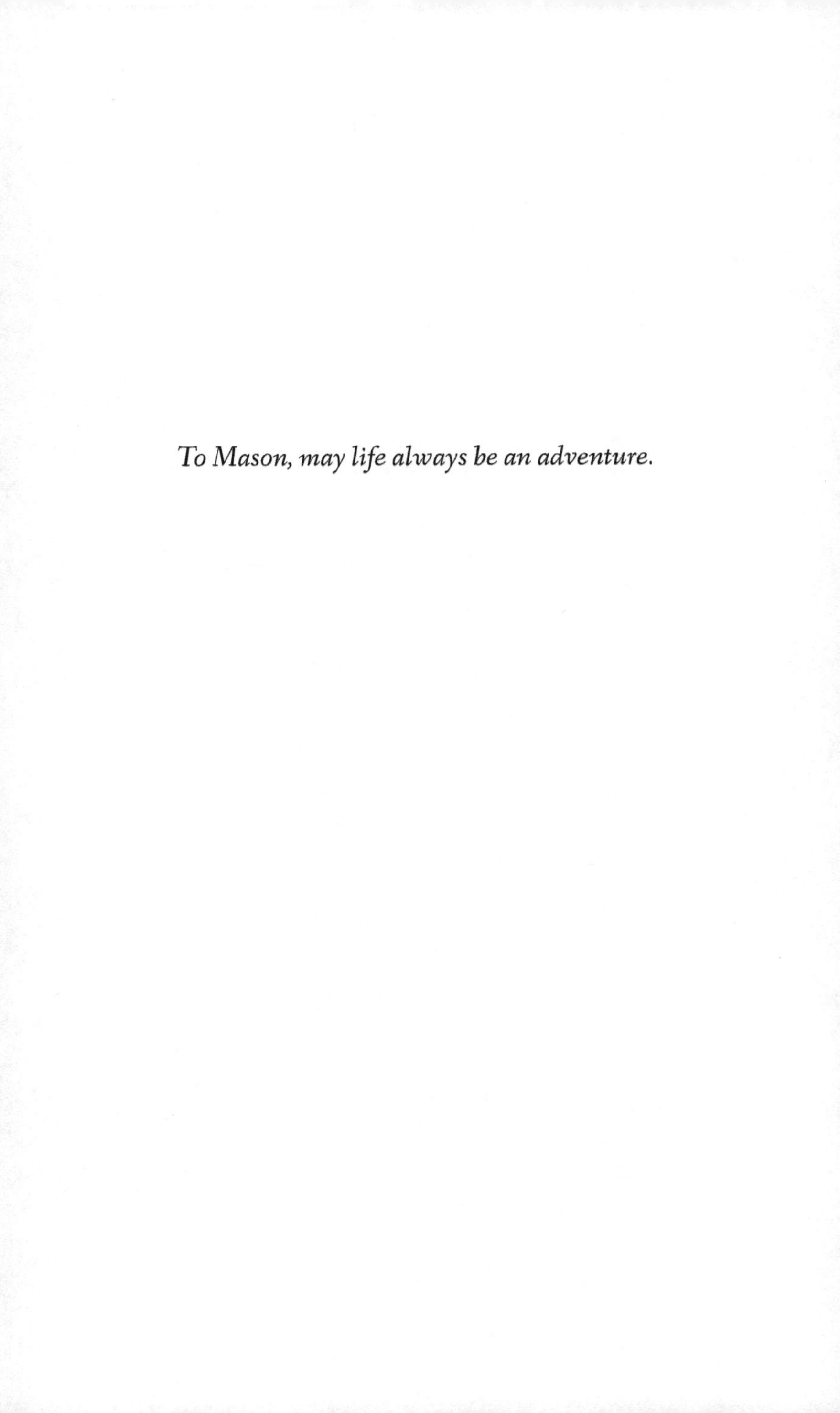

To Mason, may life always be an adventure.

Preface

"Rusted metal, bent steel, or twisted pipes, a toy you will be."

Each Fixer is born with a deep yearning to build, repair, or even create. For some, the call to invent is strong, while others spend their lives repairing things already built.

Each Fixer is allowed to determine their life's work, within their hub's limitations. While Fixers hold a higher level than the Pipes within ECHO, there are still restrictions.

But where would their world be without inventors?

Chapter 1

Home

She was furious. Her anger continued to build as she tapped her expensive boot on the wooden flooring of her office. She had spent months hunting the witness and yet nothing had come of her efforts. The only lead she had was that the Pipe Advisor Jeffson had tried to collect on the reward just after the body had been found. Jeffson had claimed they had a witness and had claimed the map found near the body was that of the crippled boy Mitch, but the doctors had ruled out the boy due to his ailment. There's no way the cripple could have been down in the tunnels, but he could have had a friend. One who Jeffson was now protecting?

She wasn't sure and grew angry each time she thought about it. Which is why she was focusing her suspicions on the two pipe boys now in the academy. One she held suspicions about knowing the witness, the other she had a deeper and more personal vendetta against.

She looked out the wide windows at what she thought of as her empire. E-carts glided along their shiny rails, and people far below went about their meaningless lives.

Her foot tapped again as she thought about the secrets she held. All of this could have been destroyed if she hadn't killed Hudson. Generations had spent their lives here, safe and secure, and the man had wanted to destroy it all, all because a machine had told him a lie.

Her reflection in the glass stared back at her, and she saw the stone-cold killer she was. Not willing to face herself, or her actions, she turned quickly away and studied the image of the young boy on her screen.

"Zane Noman," she hissed as her eyes narrowed again. "I think it's time we finally met."

I felt restless the minute I returned home from the Academy hub. I had a two-month break in my home hub, the Pipes, before level two lessons began, and I felt guilty that I was already ready to return.

At fifteen, I knew my level one training afforded me much more than many of my fellow Piper residents. But I still wouldn't be allowed down in the Pipes, the long and dangerous tunnels that fed and breathed for my home, ECHO, the Ecological Colonies Habitat Organization.

Prior to my Academy training, the only job I had been trained for was running errands for my grandmother, Mia. She ran a clothing shop from our home and kept the Piper children clothed. Mia's job provided few credits for us, but credits were limited for all Pipers.

My future possibilities were even more limited due to the mystery surrounding my father, or my lack of one. In the Pipes, children were raised and trained by family members, who showed their offspring or family relations the skills needed for the jobs held down in the tunnels. But I only had Mia. Mia, due to her sewing skills and her fear of dark tunnels, had never held a job down below our home.

It wasn't until an unknown benefactor had paid for my schooling that my future was filled with possibilities. The benefactor had paid the Academy, located two hubs away, so I could attend the school and had even provided an allowance to cover my school uniforms and equipment. He had also stipulated that Mia would keep collecting my daily child credits, something every family received for children under the age of sixteen. But we no longer worried about collecting my daily credits. I now earned my own income by selling Z-riders, a one-wheeled single-person cart I had invented. I now sold these consistently to fellow students and Academy faculty.

My three dorm mates—Rafe, Evan, and Miles—and I had run the side business of selling the Z-riders while at the Academy together. We plan to continue production of the riders and expand our business by selling them to the other hubs during school break. But when I arrived home the first day, I soon discovered Mia had made plans of her own.

Mia threw a party my first night back in my home hub. I was pleased and embarrassed to see several of my grandmother's friends arrive two hours after I had returned home from my level one graduation ceremony. The handsome white triangle pin, which I now wore on the collar of my graduation uniform, was inspected as congratulations were given.

Since our small two-room home wouldn't accommodate all of the guests at once, Mia had scheduled times for friends to come and congratulate me on my accomplishments. This way, our tidy little front room could be full of friends without bursting at its metal seams.

Two hours after the arrival of our first guest, my school

friends arrived. Evan and Miles were the first to journey to the Piper hub. Evan had a smile on his face, and Miles's usual bored expression changed to one of politeness.

I knew that Evan was used to a less-grand hub, but Miles's curiosity and shock about my less glamorous home was obvious. His dark eyes took in the room and its sparce furnishings, and I felt self-conscious about the homemade rug and slipcovers on the furniture.

"Come, let me show you some of my inventions," I quickly said, ushering both boys into my bedroom. The door curtain was drawn open, which gave the room a larger feeling but less privacy. "Here, I have a work desk."

Miles seemed to relax a bit once I showed him several of my inventions, all of which required detailed coding and electrical components, something Miles was interested in. As we were discussing my two-way talker, or TWT, Rafe came into the room.

"Well, it looks like the party is in here," he said. A broad smile flashed on his face, and his brown eyes winked out at us.

I knew that Rafe's hub, the Primer hub, was shiny and new. Its expensive homes and pretty buildings were full of high-end equipment. The Piper hub, on the other hand, was the poorest hub out of all five of the domes that made up ECHO. The homes and buildings here were only the size of sheds and were built of rusted, reused materials. Worn walkways zigged and zagged between the homes, which were built one on top of the other. People here didn't dress in expensive outfits that spoke of wealth. Instead, most people wore sturdy trousers and shirts splattered with grease or patched where they had been torn.

I felt my face heat with embarrassment. I idolized Rafe,

and now that the older boy was seeing my home, a feeling of shame crept into me.

"Are these yours?" Rafe asked. Instead of glancing at the small bedroom, he walked right up to my tiny worktable.

"Look at this! What did you call it?" Miles asked, holding up the TWT.

"It's a two-way talker." I bit my tongue before I could divulge to my friends that I had used the TWT to communicate with my best friend, Mitch.

Mitch was two years younger than me and had also grown up in the Piper hub. And just like me, he hadn't been allowed in the Pipe tunnels. But Mitch's restriction wasn't because of a missing father; it was due to his handicap. Mitch had a degenerative disease that made his legs frail, and he relied on crutches to walk.

Mitch lacked physical strength, but he excelled in his mental capabilities. Mitch was the smartest person I had ever known, and after our first year at the Academy, he still was.

But our friendship needed to remain hidden. While secretly traveling in the Pipe tunnels almost a year before, I had witnessed a murder. Since I wasn't permitted in the tunnels, Mia and I had been fearful my secret would be discovered. I had accidently left Mitch's hand-drawn map beside the body of the murdered man, which led authorities to Mitch. His handicap confirmed he wasn't the one in the tunnels that night, but that didn't stop the Forcers or the Primary from questioning him. And that was why we needed to keep our friendship a secret.

Mitch had won the lottery and been sent to the Academy right after the murder. I had wondered about my friend's luck, but later found out that Mitch's mother had been enrolling her son in the lottery every year, hoping that he would win a free education.

"Who do you talk to?" Rafe's question broke into my thoughts, and I scrambled for an answer. Coming up with nothing, I shrugged my shoulders and remained silent.

"Are they easy to make?" Evan asked.

"We could use them!" Miles perked up and started to look more closely at the square object.

We had just finished plans to build three TWT's when Mia walked in with a message pod.

"Zane, this arrived for you." She handed it to me and left us alone.

Confused by the pod, I studied it for a minute, then I clicked the flashing red light, which started the message. I felt my face grow warm when Breanna's soft voice floated out of the orb.

"Zane, I'm sorry I can't make it to your party. I just wanted to congratulate you on your level one. I hope you have a good time off, and I'll see you for level two lessons. I hope we have some classes together again."

The message ended abruptly, and the teasing from my friends started right away.

"Oh, so your girlfriend couldn't make it." Evan gave me a light punch on my arm.

"She forgot to send her love and kisses," Miles said as he looked up from the TWT schematics.

Breanna was a pretty blonde-haired, big-eyed beauty who was the first-person I had encountered at the Academy last year. We met when I stopped three boys from bullying her. Our friendship had grown when we discovered similarities in our lives.

After my friends left the party, I spent the remainder of the celebration surrounded by several of my distant family members, mostly Mia's cousins. One of these cousins was Mitch's mother, Melony Johner. When she and Mitch showed up, I ran into the back room to get a present I had made to celebrate Mitch's achievement in passing level one courses too.

I knew we still had to be careful about our hidden friendship, but since Mitch had tutored me in coding class in level one, I felt our acquaintance was justified in our own hub.

"Mitch, I wanted to thank you for all you did this last level." I handed him a large box.

"What is it?" Mitch's mother asked, her eyes filled with speculation.

Not sparing the woman a glance, I helped Mitch open the box. I was still angry at Melony for turning me in to the hub's advisor. She had convinced Advisor Jeffson that it could have been me down in the tunnels the night of the murder.

This betrayal might have cost me my credits or even resulted in me being sent to prison. Luckily, I had been protected by a man named Waltson, the very person I needed to talk to. The dying man had urged me to locate Waltson, but I had found this a difficult feat. Then, on graduation day, Rafe confirmed that his grandfather was the very gentleman I had been searching for.

"Oh, look!" Mia said as the machine I had built for Mitch was pulled from the box.

"I'm calling it a Z-roller. It's like my Z-rider, but it has four wheels to increase balance and a grip bar for steering with." I unhinged the bar, so it stood up tall. "The handles are adjustable for when you grow, and I placed a latch for your cane."

"Is it safe?" Melony asked, and I turned my eyes

towards her. When I saw concern on her face, I felt my anger at the woman soften. Despite everything, I knew Melony loved Mitch very much.

"Yes. It is slower than the Z-riders, and I also have a safety cap here for him." I reached into the bottom of the box and pulled out a bright orange cap.

Mitch wanted to try the Z-roller out right away, but I warned him that the walkways in our hub were more uneven than those found at the Academy.

"It's better to wait until you're back at school," I said with a smile.

"Then I'll wait," Mitch said with a nod as he ran a hand over the sleek machine.

The guests continued to arrive well after the evening meal hour. I didn't mind. I enjoyed seeing some of my extended family. Most were older and didn't bring their children.

Because I had been to the Academy and passed my level one classes, I was no longer considered "unemploy-able." This meant I probably wouldn't receive as much scorn from Pipers my own age. But I didn't want to find out if they would still treat me with contempt tonight, not when it was a night for celebration, so I was glad they didn't come.

When the last guest had left and it was just Mia and me, she once again put her arms around me and spoke of how proud she was.

"Now, off to bed. We can finish cleaning up tomorrow," she said when I started to pick up some plates and glasses. "Tomorrow. We will have plenty of time later," she insisted.

I slept soundly that night, my youthful mind exhausted from the day's events. I had worried my old bed wouldn't feel as soft as the one at school, but the moment my head hit the pillow, I was out.

Mia made me a special breakfast the next day, and then we set about cleaning up the chaos of the party. Halfway through the sweeping, I heard a soft knocking on the door.

"Who can that be?" Mia asked as she stood up from retrieving a fallen napkin. "The party was yesterday, not today." Her tone indicated she was concerned, and I saw her eyes sweep around the still-disorganized room.

"I'll get it," I said. I handed her the broom and opened the door to find Advisor Jeffson standing outside. His grey eyes met mine, and I tried to tamp down my fear at seeing the hub's leader.

"Advisor," Mia said quickly from behind me. She gently pushed me aside to stand in the door, successfully blocking the man from entering our home. "We are rather busy cleaning up from last night's festivities."

"Yes, Mia, I am sorry to interrupt, but I was wondering if I could have a few words with your grandson." Advisor Jeffson cast another look at me as I stood behind Mia, my palms growing sweaty with fear.

"I don't—" Mia started to say, but Jeffson quickly interrupted her.

"Please, I think he will find our conversation most profitable," Jeffson said, and a thin smile flashed on his lips.

"Well." Mia turned to me, and I gave her a slight nod. My curiosity was piqued by the man's request. "Fine, but my house has not yet been set right." She opened the door further to let him in.

"It's fine, lovely," Advisor Jeffson added with another smile, but his eyes remained on me.

"Please, sit. Can I get you some caffeine substitute?" Mia politely asked.

"No, I don't want to be a bother. I was just hoping for a quick word with Zane," Jeffson said as he sat on Mia's couch.

Awkward silence filled the small room as Mia and I continued to look down upon the Pipe's advisor, who seemed content to sit there in silence. I cleared my throat and raised my eyebrows.

"Ah, I, that is," Jeffson said, and I got the impression the man was nervous about something. "With recent developments, I was wondering if you might be interested in a position."

Position? I wondered if I had heard the advisor wrong. The last time I had seen this man, he had accused me of being down in the tunnels and withholding information regarding the murder. Only a call from the unknown Waltson stopped the advisor from continuing his angry accusation. This had all taken place in front of the Primary's advisor, Davis Elliotson.

"Position? What position?" Mia quickly asked as she drew closer to me.

"Um, well, as you know, your grandson is one of only two who have been privileged to attend the Academy from our hub. Given his new stature, and education, I hoped he would come and work for my office." Advisor Jeffson continued to look up at me as I stood behind Mia.

"Work?' Mia turned to look at me, a confused look on her face.

"Of course, you would have an income," Advisor Jeffson quickly continued. "And there would be no need to return to the Academy, as the position only requires a level one." He quickly stood. "You would also be provided with a room in the main tower," Jeffson continued, and I had a fleeting vision of the tall building in the center of the hub.

"A room?" Mia asked as she continued to look at me.

My mind whirled with possibilities. Here was an opportunity that I would have never had prior to being gifted the chance at an education. A job! An actual job was being presented to me, Zane Noman, a fatherless orphan who hadn't even been allowed to practice a basic job in my own hub.

"Yes. The official title would be counselor, a high position with many benefits," he continued quickly as if afraid to allow any time between his words, fearful maybe of a rejection. "Included are health privileges and meals."

Mia held up a hand as her eyes finally turned to Advisor Jeffson. "Am I to understand that this position is being offered to Zane because he graduated level one?"

"Of course," Jeffson said with shock. "You must understand that we have no record of any Pipers going to the Academy. And here we are now, blessed quite unexpectedly with two boys, both who have passed their first level."

"So have you offered Mitch Frankson a job also?" I asked, excited for my friend, who also had been limited in his future possibilities because of his physical disability.

"Well..." Jeffson looked uncomfortable all of a sudden, and his eyes turned away from me as he returned to sit on the couch. "Mitch, that is, he has decided to return to school and obtain further levels."

"He said no?" I asked with a smile. It was just like him having a plan that would allow him to continue to use the free education provided by the lottery. Knowing Mitch, he aimed to gain as high of a level as the lottery would allow and then continue seeking advancements beyond even that which an education could provide.

"He indicated he wished to continue with his education," Advisor Jeffson said with a nod.

"Advisor, I think Zane and I will need some time to consider your offer," Mia said. She folded her hands as she studied the man.

"Actually," I said, stepping forward, "I don't need any time."

<h1 style="text-align:center">Chapter 2</h1>

<hr>

<h2 style="text-align:center">Work</h2>

"**A**re you sure?" Mia asked me, and I saw the concern on her face.

After Advisor Jeffson had left, my grandmother faced me, no doubt worried I was missing a great opportunity that would assure me a promising future. But I knew what I wanted now, and it was more than what the Pipe hub could offer me.

"Mia, a counselor is one of the lowest jobs available for clerks." I looked into her worried eyes, shocked to realize I had grown taller than her. I marveled at the thought that soon I might tower over her. "The credits for that job are less than what I'm earning now building my Z-riders. And I would have to give up school, give up any hope of promotion with only a level one certificate."

"So," Mia asked hesitantly, "you are enjoying your education?"

I pondered her question for a few seconds. Was I enjoying school? Of course, I was. I didn't like certain aspects of it, the amount of homework being the first thing that came to my mind. But then I thought of my friends, my bunk mates, and even my professors. A smile crossed my lips when Breanna's face flashed in my mind's eye.

"Yes," I finally replied. "I'm enjoying it quite a bit. But most importantly, it will allow me to provide for both of us." When Mia looked confused, I quickly continued, "Mia, I have only one level so far. Imagine what I could do with a level five or six."

"You intend to gain that many levels?" Mia asked with a smile.

"I will go as far as my benefactor allows me to." I pulled her toward the couch so we could sit and talk. "Speaking of..."

I then told her about my theories regarding the donor. I explained why I believed Adam Waltson, who happened to be the grandfather of my friend Rafe, was the unknown donor. I also told her that I knew Rafe's father, Hudson Adamson, had been the man who had died in the tunnels almost a year ago.

"Someone from the main hub was in the tunnels?" Mia asked, and a small wrinkle formed between her brows.

"I asked Rafe what his dad did for a job, and I looked up his grandfather. But the titles and job descriptions are confusing. I hope to discover more. Maybe Mitch can help me understand them." I shrugged my shoulders. "I know 'Controller' is Waltson's title, but I don't know what that entails or why Rafe's father was down in the tunnels."

Mia had many questions that I didn't have answers to. I felt the same worry I saw now in her eyes and when she started to rub her temples, I tried to appease her with a promise that I would continue to research Adam Waltson.

"Look, my level education is assured. As long as I show up, the Academy will take me. If Adam Waltson is the person paying, I don't know why, nor do I know if he knows about me witnessing his son's death. But I am friends with Rafe, and I will continue to hide the fact that I was in the tunnels the night his dad died."

With a nod, Mia finally stood, and we finished cleaning up the party mess. Before we had finished, however, another knock sounded on the door, and I was pleased to see Evan again.

"I thought it would be faster to come and visit than send a message pod," Evan said with a smile.

"I just saw you last night!" I returned his smile as I waved him into the now clean front room.

"Yeah, but last night was for fun. This is business," Evan explained as he sat down. "Before yesterday's party, my dad told me of a workshop that has become available. Before I came today, I went over and looked at it. Zane, it would be perfect for us!" The excitement in Evan's tone made his voice two octaves higher than usual. His dark eyes were bright as he leaned forward towards me.

"Workshop?" Mia asked as she brought drinks out for us and set them on the small table.

"Yeah, you know, to build the Z-riders." Evan took the cup Mia handed him. "It's in the Fixer hub, but it has a small loft you can use to sleep in, if you want to," Evan said as he studied me.

"Do you think we need a workshop? I mean, I was just going to build some here at home."

"But Z, we have over thirty orders just this week. You can't expect to fill those orders if we're all working in different hubs," Evan said with a shake of his dark head. "This way, we are all in one location and can keep our equipment and tools in the shop."

"But won't that cost credits?" Mia asked as she sat next to me on the couch.

"Sure, it will but I've calculated that into our profits, and having the workshop will allow us to fill more orders. Plus, when we're at school, my dad will take over the rent and use the workshop for his inventions," Evan explained.

I felt Evan's excitement now as possibilities filled my mind. Almost two whole months of building Z-riders would increase our profits, and those were earnings Mia, and I could use. I knew the three other boys didn't rely on the credits from the Z-riders like I did, with the exception of Evan, who was saving for his own E-cart.

"If you have time, I could show you the workshop now." Evan turned his questioning eyes on Mia.

"Oh, I think I will leave this to Zane," she said with a wink. "Besides, I have a friend coming over, who will also be here for dinner." Mia turned to me. "You remember Forcer Carrington?"

At the name, my mind went blank. Then an image of the large man who had helped rescue Mia and me from Weston and his cronies flashed in my mind.

"The Forcer from the main hub?" I asked, and a pink shade crept up Mia's face.

"Run along, just be back before seventeen hundred," she said instead of responding to my question. She quickly ushered us out of the house.

Evan had ridden his Z-rider to my hub, but because of the uneven walkways in the Pipe dome, we had to walk to the connecting tunnels before we could use the riders safely.

The rush of adrenaline kicked in for me when we passed out of the tunnel and into the main hub. I didn't know if it was the brighter lights or fresh air, but either way, a smile flashed across my face as I raced behind Evan.

The workshop was a large, attached shed located

behind two homes. It was nestled high up against the back wall of the Fixer hub, but I thought it was great.

"This place is bigger than Mia's whole house," I exclaimed as I studied the space. There were two broken tables in the empty room and a metal ladder that led to the sleeping loft. A bathroom with a dingy shower was nestled under the loft, which was in need of repairs and good cleaning.

"So, do you think this will work?" Evan asked, and I heard hope in his voice.

"Evan, are you sure we can afford this?" I asked after I studied the workshop twice.

Evan gave a nod of his dark head, and his eyes swept across the room. "We have enough credits in the business savings, and if we fill our orders more quickly, then we can double our income before school starts again. Then Dad will take over while we're in school. Honestly, he's been looking for a workshop because Mom's been complaining about his clutter around the house." The smile he flashed me was wide.

"When can we move in?" I returned Evan's grin as my own excitement grew.

Five days after we signed the agreement, the workshop was ours. We all brought our partially built Z-riders and placed them in a neat line along one table. Rafe had brought two stools, and Miles had supplied a long table. The room still looked bare, but that would soon change.

"Are you sure you have the list?" I asked Rafe as we locked the door to our new shop. We each carried our Z-rider except Evan, who was going to take his mom's E-cart so we could bring back our purchases. Today was shopping day.

"You already asked me that," Rafe said as he set his rider on the ground. "I know it's your first time going to the Printer hub, but don't act so nervous. It's just another hub."

"Yeah, you act as if we're going underground again," Miles said, sure to whisper the last two words.

My friends had kept our adventure of that night several months ago secret, but between us we had all started to exaggerate our voyage. We now called the Pipes the 'underground,' but the scary parts of that night had somehow turned into an adventuresome and daring mission.

"He hasn't been to the Printers yet," Evan said with a shake of his dark head. "Don't worry, it's a little like the Fixers, but crazier." He smiled.

When we arrived at the Printer hub, I was enthralled. One side of the dome contained enormous stacks of used and discarded items from all five hubs. Large mounds of dark metal twisted into odd shapes were stacked in high piles, some reaching all the way to the top of the sphere.

This hub also contained impressive printers. These large white machines had fences surrounding them and only the printing technicians were allowed inside. Each fence had a hut where purchases could be ordered. These weren't food printers or even the small printers each hub held for emergency items. These were fully functioning ULTAC printers.

I stared at the large, boxy machines and saw how the raw materials were fed into input bays at one side of the printer. Technicians worked on the numerous controls and screens, and there was a long line of people waiting to fill their orders.

"Look over there. That's where they break down the

materials." Evan tugged on my arm and pointed far to the left. "We have to get the permit first, then we can go into the piles and start our search."

I followed Evan to an odd square building that sat in a large bare lot two blocks from the printers. A flat fee was paid, and then we each were issued a permit along with one red helmet and a plastic vest to be worn while we were in the scrap yards.

"It helps ensure the machines see us," Evan explained as we moved beyond the gate into the scrapyard. "See." He pointed upwards.

Up on the dome ceiling, I saw rails running along the curve. Each rail had odd claws and buckets, which zipped around collecting the materials.

"They are run by technicians in another building, but the red of our helmets shows up on their monitors, so they don't scoop us up with a pile of materials."

Despite Evan's assurance, I had a fleeting image of being picked up by one of the large buckets and dismantled piece by piece. After a hard shove from Rafe, I put that image in the back of my mind and followed my friends to the first pile.

"The control panels are over there," Rafe advised. "Why don't you and Miles find them while Evan and I look for tires." He ripped the carefully printed list in half and gave me the bottom, which contained gears, switches, and electrical boards we would need.

Three hours later, I was filthy and sweaty, but we had found more than enough of the items on our list.

"Let's take these back to the cart and see how the others are doing," Miles suggested. When we got there, I saw Evan was as dirty as I felt.

Rafe and Evan had also had luck. Most of the tires were

similar in shape and size. Some had already been loaded into the cart, while others sat in a neat pile next to it.

"We only need four smaller ones, as we have a special order for another Z-roller," Rafe said with a smile. "But to be safe, we should grab eight more."

We spent a total of four hours rummaging in the large piles of discarded wheels and metals on the recycling side of the hub that day. The sounds and smells were intense, and I was glad to get back to the Fixer hub that evening. I had told Mia that I would be spending the night at the workshop, so I wasn't worried about the time, until Rafe announced he had to go home.

"Mom has a special dinner planned tomorrow, and I'm expected to attend," Rafe said with a shrug of his shoulders. "I expect Breanna and her mom will be there."

Shocked, I turned to study the older boy. "Breanna is going to your house?"

"Yeah, well, my mom is pretty high up in the main office, and the Primary knew my dad. I guess they went to the Academy together or something. Anyway, it's not the first time she's attended one of Mom's parties."

It was still odd for me to think that Breanna and Rafe grew up so close to each other. Now I realized the closeness wasn't just because they came from the same hub. They were in the same social circle as well.

"Want me to say hi for you?" Rafe asked in a teasing voice.

I dipped my head and gave a quick nod, then I quickly turned to unroll the blankets Mia had packed for me. The small cot Miles had borrowed from one of the medical clinics sat against the far wall. We were all going to take turns sleeping in the workshop. Evan had explained that, without a stronger door and lock, our items might be "nicked" by others for their own inventions.

"Might as well add a business sign," Evan said as he measured the door frame.

"And we need to replace the stairs leading up to the small room," I said as we all stood in the doorway and looked at the rusted metal railing and steps. The steps alone had prevented me from moving the cot upstairs. One false move and you might end up back on the main floor more quickly than you wanted.

Evan and Miles didn't remain much longer after Rafe had left. As I said goodbye to Evan, I noticed the hub's lights were starting to dim for the night. I gave Evan and Miles a wave and watched them disappear down the lane. Miles was on his Z-rider, and Evan was leisurely walking to his family's home.

I remained in the doorway for a bit and was just about to turn back into the workshop when I saw a familiar figure.

The old man, Adam Waltson, had just appeared from around a corner only one block from the workshop. He didn't give any indication that he'd seen me as he hurried down the street towards the connecting tunnel.

The urge to follow him was overwhelming, but I knew I couldn't leave the shop, not until it was secure better.

Disappointment filled me as I watched the bent form of the old man disappear behind a corner. I stood there, watching the Fixer hub grow dark, while questions filled my mind about Adam.

Before I shut the door on the darkness, I wondered briefly why Adam would be wandering inside the Fixer hub at such a late hour.

Chapter 3

Progress

"It should have all five hubs," Evan interjected as he leaned over the table and grabbed the tablet from Miles. "Here, see, five circles then..."

"But it's the Pipes we need to represent." Rafe's strong objection had me peeking over the banister. I was trying to secure the flooring and thought the others were working on the stairs until their argument caught my attention.

"What are you three doing?" I asked. Their tools had been abandoned for the tablet Evan currently held in his hands.

"Nothing." Miles moved back towards the stairs.

"He should know. After all, he's the one who started it." Rafe looked up at me, his face set and his dark brows drawn together. "Z, come on down here for a minute."

Wiping the dust off my hands, I made my way carefully down the half-repaired stairs. I caught a quick glance of the drawing on the tablet, and my confusion increased. "What's going on?"

It was Rafe who answered, but only after he had placed

his hand on my shoulder and looked me squarely in the eyes.

"Z, there's a growing movement. One you should know about," Rafe said. He turned to study Miles.

"Yeah, well, I kind of told my parents about our questions. You know, about how the Pipers don't have child limitations." Miles shrugged his skinny shoulders. "Anyway, that got my mom thinking, and when I told her what you said about how the kids in the Piper hub are required to go down into the tunnels, and how some don't come back…"

I had never heard Miles speak so much about anything that wasn't related to coding. First, I was shocked, then dread filled me as Mitch's warnings came back to me. I had cautioned the others not to bring up these differences because it could only mean trouble. Mitch had convinced me that change could only come from the Primer hub, the hub that ran the government of my world.

Now as my friends spoke of how they had each talked to their parents about their discoveries, my fear was mixed with pride. They had listened, and they all felt passionate about the dangers a Piper faced each day.

"We told other students too, and my parents are speaking about it in my hub," Evan said, his dark eyes studying me as he spoke. "Z, this injustice has to stop."

"But how?" I asked, studying them all. "If the Pipers don't go into the tunnels, ECHO will die. We will all die," I said with a shake of my head. "I appreciate what you feel." I waved my hands in the air while still holding the metal tubing I had used to bang some of the rusty nails back into place on the landing. "But we can't change ECHO without causing damage."

"That's it!" Miles shouted, grabbing the tablet from Rafe. He bent over and, within seconds, turned the tablet to face all of us, a grin on his usually pouting face. "Here, the symbol of the Pipes."

The sketch was crude, but even I could see what it represented—a fist thrusted up, a broken pipe held tight. A blue circle representing the Piper hub encircled the image.

"Z, the movement has already started. Even we can't stop it now." Rafe placed a hand on my shoulder again. "All we can do is try and help shape where this revolution goes."

"But Rafe, I fear it will end in disaster," I said with a shake of my head. Nothing I said persuaded them to set aside their revolution, so I returned up the stairs to finish my work on the landing.

I heard them agree to Mile's drawing. When they started working on the steps again, I sat down on the metal slabs and studied my hands, deep in thought.

Revolution. Movement. These words struck me as I thought of my home hub. How could the world of ECHO continue to live if the Pipers weren't willing to put their lives in danger every day by traversing the tunnels? I thought of my time in the tunnels, how I had traveled in them secretly every night until that fateful time when I had witnessed the murder of Rafe's father.

My friends didn't know I had been there. No one except my grandmother and my best friend Mitch knew. I hoped no one else would ever know.

I turned when Rafe came and sat on the ground next to me. He had a smear of grease on his left cheek, and his hair was disheveled.

"Z," he said, and his eyes dropped to his own hands. "I wanted to tell you what my mother said when I told her... Well, you know." His shoulders slumped before he continued. "She knew."

I sat silently as Rafe's words sunk in. When I said nothing, he continued.

"She told me that the Pipers were none of my business. As a Primer, I should only be concerned with my education, and that it was the government's job to administer the hubs. She also reminded me that ECHO had been running smoothly for generations." Rafe flexed his fingers and made a fist. When he punched the metal flooring next to him, the others on the stairs stopped working. "Z, she warned me to not speak of the segregation, of your hub's struggles, to anyone."

"You think the Primer hub knows?" I asked. "That even the Primer herself knows the dangers the people in my hub face?"

"I know she does." Rafe looked back up at me. "I asked Breanna."

Just the mention of the girl's name had my heart racing, but I stamped down my feelings and looked back at Rafe. "She told you?"

He nodded and sighed before continuing. "She asked her mother, and she too was warned after her mother tried to brush off her questions."

"Sounds like your girlfriend has some guts," Evan said from the top of the stairs.

"She's the one leading the movement in the Primer hub," Rafe said with a smile. "She keeps bossing me around and is the one who wanted the symbol before nightfall."

Revolution. I pondered the word as I went home to Mia that night deep in thought. Could a symbol and a few kids really change how my people lived their lives? If so, what would that change look like? What could it mean for my world?

With my head hung low, I walked through the front door and saw Mia. She was bent over her new sewing machine as she hummed and tapped her foot to the music coming out of the transistor.

"Dinner will be ready as soon as I finish this shirt." She waved a hand at me as I continued walking to my room.

Three new inventions littered my desk and part of a half-dissected flashbulb lay on my bed. Throwing that on the floor, I plopped down and kicked off my shoes.

I had spent two whole days in the Fixer hub building Z-riders and trying to talk my friends out of starting a rebellion. But the only outcome had been the completion of ten new Z-riders.

Rafe had insisted that they were only speaking to close friends about the Pipes. Breanna had to keep her involvement quiet, so she only contacted him once or twice a week with ideas.

I shook my head and looked at the patches on my ceiling as a smile crossed my lips. Breanna was good at organization and making lists.

A faint beeping distracted me, and I looked over at my school tablet to see the message light blinking. Hoping it was a message from Breanna, I leaned over and grabbed the device.

It wasn't Breanna, but ten more orders for riders, two for Z-rollers, and a call from a food mart in the main hub who wanted to place an advertisement for their store on my riders.

I sent the orders to the others and pondered the last request. Advertisements?

So far all of our orders have been from word of mouth. People saw others riding their Z-riders and asked them about the machines. If we advertised, this could double our orders. An idea started to form in my brain.

I spent the next twenty minutes at my desk, drawing up and creating an E-page. I had to run this idea past the others, so when I was done, I sent my draft to them for their opinion.

After dinner, I had their reply.

"Great idea," Evan had typed.

"I'll get prices," Rafe offered. And Miles gave a solid thumbs up with a rough sketch of a Z-rider with the words "Z-ride into the future" written above it.

Before the week was up, we had two E-boards flashing in the main hub and one in both the Fixer and Printer hubs. Within hours, we had over fifty new orders.

Three days later I had moved to the Fixer hub in the hopes that most of the orders would be completed before school started again. Almost three weeks had passed since school had let out, so my break was almost half over. Evan stayed with me at the workshop, but Miles's and Rafe's parents insisted they remain in their own hub. They had day passes that allowed them to travel back and forth but could only commit to coming every other day.

The loft had been repaired and a new door and lock ensured our tools and supplies were safe. I kept busy during the day making the riders but kept an eye out for the mysterious Waltson.

I hadn't seen the man since my first night in the Fixer hub, but something told me I would see him again soon.

I still hadn't talked to Rafe about my suspicions, nor did I ask him any more questions about his grandfather. I didn't want to raise any red flags by asking too much about the man. Instead, I talked to him about his father once or twice.

I would broach the subject only when Rafe brought up his dad.

"Dad showed me how to do this," Rafe would say, and I would always pounce in with questions like "What was he like?"

Rafe loved to talk about his late father but part of me always felt guilty after these conversations. If Rafe knew that I had witnessed his father's demise, would he even be my friend?

Two days after I moved into the Fixer hub, I had a video call from the main hub about an E-board.

"Sorry to bother you, sir," a man named Swanson said over the line. He had a round face with a pencil thin mustache over his top lip and light blue eyes staring back at them. "We had some issues and one of your boards was defaced."

"Defaced?" I turned to study Evan, who shrugged his shoulders as he bent over to pop a wheel onto one of the machines we were working on.

"Ah, yes, well, there is a faction who has been going around spraying messages over our boards. We can replace the board, but it will take another day to manufacture," the man explained.

"A faction?" I asked, confused by his term. I had no idea what a faction was and could only come up with math figures.

"These Pipers," Mr. Swanson said, and my blood turned cold. "We have seen this symbol on most of our boards recently. But not to worry, I can have the sign replaced."

"Um," I said as Evan rushed over to me.

"Is the sign ruined?" Evan asked as he pushed me out of the way.

"Well, no. The symbol only appears on the lower half of your advertisement," Mr. Swanson replied.

"Most of our signs are only up for another two days," Evan said as he looked down at his chart, which showed our timeframes and orders. "We all return to the Academy in less than four weeks and therefore kept our advertisements limited. If the sign isn't too badly damaged, there is no need for your company to pay for another one."

The smile Evan gave the man was both charming and friendly. Mr. Swanson was pleased to hear this and showed his appreciation by giving us a discount on our next E-board.

I was still shaken, even after Evan hung up on the man. Evan's smile fell away, and he shook his head. "Z, I'm sorry man. It was my idea to spray our own signs. We didn't want to tag every other sign and leave ours. That would have been very suspicious."

"Tag?" I croaked, sitting in the nearest chair.

"Yeah. Well, Rafe and Miles are doing most of it. They can draw better than me. They got most of the signs up two nights ago, but I had them go back out and tag at least one of ours. It's in the main hub, one near the outer wall."

"Evan, you're telling me Rafe and Miles have been sneaking around painting that symbol." I pointed to where Evan, Rafe, and Miles had stood several days ago when they had come up with the image of the fist holding the pipe. "They've been spreading it?"

"Well, yeah," Evan said as he scratched his stubbly chin. "You can't start a revolution without spreading the word about your cause." He shook his head and continued his work on the rider.

Chapter 4

Deception

I had mixed emotions about the actions of my friends. On the one hand, I knew their intentions were just. They felt passionate about my hub being treated unfairly. Children working in the tunnels, and men and women putting their lives in danger for measly few credits a day. Then there were the living conditions we Pipers resided in.

Rafe and the others said they had used their visit the day of my party to examine the Pipe hub. I felt ashamed at first, when they explained how sad my home looked to them. Their description of my hub had me seeing it in a new light.

Children in torn clothing, walkways that were mismatched and unsafe, homes with leaning walls or missing doors. Men and women who looked tired, sad, and ill. These were all common in the Piper hub. Evan and Miles had said they had felt saddened by what they saw, which caused my defenses to rise.

"We have some good qualities, things you missed on your short visit," I said, crossing my arms over my chest.

"We know that." Miles stood in front of the others. "But you have to understand, we only see the pain and suffering your hub endures. Remember how little a Piper earns for their hard and dangerous work."

Miles's words still echoed in my ears when we ran to the Printers hub two days later. We needed new supplies for our increasing number of orders and while Evan and his dad worked on the riders, Miles and I ran to pick up more tires and boards.

We rode our E-cart to the main hub and then passed down the long tunnel leading to the Printer hub. The Forcers had questions about my pass, but after Miles showed him the work order, they finally let me through.

"I don't know what their issue was," Miles said as he cast a look over his shoulder. "We've been here once already this month."

Shrugging my shoulders, I pulled out our supply list and focused on finding the right gates. I parked the cart near the check-in office. "The tires are here; I'll find them if you want to look for the circuits again."

Miles gave me a nod, but his frown was causing a line between his brows. I studied him until he nodded again and turned off towards the circuits.

I spent two hours finding the right tires. Most of the ones I found were too bald, and I worried we might need to pay some credits and have new tires printed next time.

I was loading up the last of the tires, which I had tied together with a small rope to keep them from falling off the cart, when I heard a small cough behind me. Thinking it was Miles, I kept piling the tires in the cart and grumbled at my friend over my shoulders. "Give me a hand. These tires are zapping my nerves."

When a pair of small hands reached over and grabbed

the rope, I dropped the last tire right on my foot. As I hopped around, spouting a few choice words that would have made Mia scold me, I saw a small dark-haired woman standing next to the E-cart, watching me. She had odd-shaped eyes under thick long bangs and despite the fact that she was wearing an ill-fitting jumper with the logo of Printers on it, I got the impression from the way she stood that she wasn't really used to manual labor. She had only one hand on the rope holding the tires in the back seat. Her other hand was on her small hip. The frown on her lips didn't touch the rest of her pretty face, and I thought I saw speculation in her dark eyes.

"Oh, sorry," I said as I rubbed the top of my sore foot. "I thought you were my friend."

She said nothing and continued to study me. Feeling self-conscious, I cleared my throat and bent to lift the tire that had all but crushed my right foot.

"Um, thanks for helping," I said, and lifted the tire into the pile. I tried to grab the rope from her, but she stood there unmoving, one finger on the knot. "Um..."

"Do you have a permit for these." Her voice was smooth, but her tone caused a tickle in the back of my mind. Annoyance soon took over.

"I have a work order," I said as I tried to balance the tire on the back of the cart. She still hadn't released the rope, and I was worried the whole pile was going to come crashing down on my already aching foot.

"May I see it?"

I narrowed my eyes at her. Was she young or old? I couldn't tell, as she had no wrinkles around the eyes and her small body was hidden under the jumper. She could have been ten years old or thirty. Either way, she was holding me hostage until I showed her the work order, a piece of paper that I now realized Miles had with him clear across the hub.

"Sure, Miles has it. He can show you when he gets here." I reached for the rope again.

She slammed her hand flat on the rope, and my patience wore even thinner. When she made no move to aid me, I finally pulled the tire off the top of the pile and set it slowly next to my feet. "Look, we had to show it to the Forcers when we came in. My friend Miles was the one holding it, and he's over in the other gate. We have several large orders to fill, and I was stuck getting the tires." My words caused no movement from her. Her dark eyes were the only thing that moved as they looked from my face to the full cart and back to me.

"I promise, Miles has the order." I placed my hands on my hips.

"Then I suggest you run along and find your friend." She kept her hand on the rope.

"What's the issue?" I asked. My voice sounded too high, and she narrowed her eyes at me. "Before we leave, we have to show the work order to the attendant."

Still nothing from the woman. Finally giving in, I sighed and turned to make my way towards where I had last seen Miles. Unfortunately, he wasn't there. I passed three gates and two small attendant huts before I found him. I grabbed an arm full of boards and the work order from him and returned to the cart, but the woman wasn't there.

Frowning, I threw the boards in the front seat and walked around the cart, looking for her. Finally giving up, I shoved the work order in my pocket and threw the last tire into the pile. I tied it into place, uttering a few more choice words, and then marched back to where Miles was.

"Didn't even bother to stick around," I grumbled as I helped him.

"Who?" Miles asked as he bent over to retrieve a discarded memory board.

"Some female worker. She demanded to see our work order, but when I went back with it, she was gone," I said with a frown.

"Was she pretty?" Miles asked, his eyes questioning. Miles had recently been obsessed with finding a girlfriend. He had taken to thinking about any girl he saw as a potential love interest. I thought this had to do with Evan's recent new friend Bailey, a pretty mixed-raced girl with large eyes and full lips. She was a friend of Asher, Rafe's girlfriend. Asher had introduced Bailey to Evan right after the graduation ceremony.

"I don't know, I wasn't paying attention to that. She was small and bossy though." I bent to help locate five more memory boards before we left.

Building Z-riders was exhausting and dirty work. Evan and I spent most of our days bent over the workshop tables, throwing the riders together. We had a system where Evan put the wheels on while I programed the memory boards using a secondhand computer Evan's dad had bought.

I traveled home only once during the second month of break but planned to return home right before school started. But spending my days and nights in the Fixer hub had its advantages. Evan's mom wasn't much for cooking, so most of my meals came from the hub's printers. Eating meal hash and running around the Pipe hub had kept me skinny. Now I was stuffing my face with noodles and printed protein squares. I had a new addiction to fried crisps and had grown an inch taller. My arms had bulked up too from lifting tires on a daily basis.

I needed a haircut before the month was over, and Evan suggested I use his barber. This was my first professional haircut, and I was excited until I got back to the workshop and realized the man had cut the hair around my ears a bit too short. Now I felt my ears looked too large, and I missed how Mia had always trimmed my hair just the way I liked it. Plus, I missed the ten credits it had cost me.

When not working on the Z-riders, I spent my free time walking the Fixer hub. I was fascinated by the inventions that littered the streets and walkways of this hub. Most were still a work in progress, but there were several that had been abandoned. Some were too large for the Leviathan—the machine Evan's dad had built to get rid of unwanted inventions from the streets—to remove. Evan's dad had tried to remove several inventions by dismantling them, but for each one he removed, two more would be abandoned.

I found the passion for invention in this hub fascinating. The Fixers were interested in creating everything from toenail clippers to huge machines made to repair the cracks in the walls of the skyscrapers.

Twice more I thought I caught a glimpse of Adam Waltson. The second time I saw him it was out of the corner of my eye while walking with Evan towards his parents' home. I couldn't leave Evan to follow the man, so I had to settle for craning my neck to see which way he had gone. When I located the street the following day, I was disappointed to discover a dead end.

The next time I was alone and quickly chased after Waltson. For an old man, he sure moved quickly. I followed him up three flights of stairs towards the back wall of the hub. We snaked in and out of corridors of townhomes and back down a narrow stairwell leading towards the higher homes along the wall's edge before I lost him again.

To my frustration, neither the stairs nor walkways went anywhere that could explain his quick disappearance. I thought again of asking Rafe about his grandfather, but my friend was growing quite suspicious of all my questions.

Since this chase had taken place close to nighttime, I started spending my free evenings wandering the hub, much like I had done down in the tunnels of the Pipes. I always had my Z-rider strapped to my back for when I grew tired of walking.

My ability to internally map out streets and locations helped me understand the ins and outs of this new hub quickly.

It wasn't long before school started again and understood that this free time would soon come to an end. Being fifteen now, I felt very mature and grown up. So when I felt a tickle of fear creep into me one night, it stopped me in my tracks.

I had just passed a large monster of a machine that had been built to resemble a mythical creature called a whale when the hair on the back of my neck stood up. Spinning quickly, I noticed that the overhead lights had already been dimmed for the night.

I studied the dark road behind me and saw no one. The faint lights showed only abandoned inventions littering the way. But my feeling of unease grew.

My breath came in short, quick explosions and my palms grew damp as I stood there like an idiot. There was no sound, no movement behind me, and no explanation for my feelings. But that didn't stop me from being scared.

When I heard a pop, it sounded as loud as an explosion, and I was jolted. I stumbled back over a discarded pipe and fell backwards. As I hit the hard metal flooring, my mind raced back to that fateful night in the tunnels when I had witnessed the death of Hudson Adamson.

This comparison was too much for my terrified mind, and I scrambled up and raced behind the closest machine. My heart was trying to escape my chest, and the air inside the hub no longer seemed adequate for my lungs. I flipped off my chest plate's lights and reached for the only weapon I had—a large wrench that was attached to the device I was hiding behind.

I thought I heard a faint scrape, but when I peeked around the corner of the machine, I saw nothing. Not wanting to move from my hiding place, I remained there until my sweat cooled and I started to shiver.

"You're being stupid," I hissed to myself, but I still wasn't willing to expose myself. Something deep inside told me I was in danger, and I knew better than to ignore my inner voice.

I would eventually have to leave, to flee to safety, and I decided my Z-rider was the fastest way to do that. But that would require me to turn my lights on so I could see the roadway. This might mean the danger could see me too.

It was then that I saw the gaping doorway to my right. A faint far-off light beyond showed a long corridor that I could escape down. Slowly and as quietly as I could, I moved towards the door and hopefully safety.

When a light flashed far beyond my safe hiding place, I raced towards the doorway. My heartbeat was so loud in my ears that I couldn't tell if there were any sounds of pursuit, but I ran as if I were being chased by an army.

The corridor led away from the street and down into the backside of homes. I hadn't been inside this hallway before, so I hoped it would come out on the other side of the tall townhomes on this street. When I reached the single lightbulb, I had spotted, I cast a quick glance over my shoulder and saw that the door I had entered had been shut behind me.

Not remembering if I had closed it, I kept a fast pace and switched on my chest plate lights again. Dust covered the floor, and with each of my steps a puff of dirt rose and clogged my mouth and nose. But still I ran.

There was only one way forward, but eventually I reached a steep set of stairs leading down. I lost count after fifty and started to worry I was heading down into the tunnels below the hub, but finally the path leveled off again.

I glanced at my plate's clock and saw that only ten minutes had passed. When I came to the door, I hesitated and cast another look over my shoulder.

Where did this lead to? I reached out and tugged on the handle. The door opened quietly, and I felt a blast of fresh air meet me. When I walked into the room, my mouth dropped open and then a smile formed on my lips.

The hidden room was filled from floor to high ceiling with monitors showing various streets and walkways inside the Fixer hub.

Chapter 5

Revolution

Four days before school started, I intended to return to my home hub. I wanted to spend time with Mia and gather my supplies before heading back to the Academy.

I hadn't told any of my friends about the secret monitor room, nor did I intend to. When I had returned to the workshop that night, Evan had asked where I had been. I had lied and told him that I had gotten lost and went quickly to bed. I didn't know why I wanted to keep the hidden room to myself, but I had a strong urge to keep this, and my fear of danger that night, secret. I wasn't sure if it was shame of my fear or the possibility of danger that kept me quiet.

I didn't have a chance to return to the room the next day, but I was able to go back two days later, once again after dark. I was disappointed when I discovered the door locked. There was no knob or keyhole, and so I stood outside the door to the long hallway feeling defeated and disappointed.

I went back two more times before I gave up hope of reentering the secret room. But I wondered if there were similar rooms like this in the other hubs. I made a promise to myself to look and hopefully discover all of ECHO's secrets, if I could.

We still had orders coming in for Z-riders, but a new warning on our E-page explained that there was a considerable delay in filling purchases, and it allowed the customer to place their name on a waiting list.

I checked the page each day and confirmed that orders had slowed considerably since we had taken down our advertising signs. I went to the hub's page and was filling out a request to return home when a warning came up.

"Due to a contamination, no passes to the Pipe hub will be allowed until further notice." It flashed across my screen, and I leaned closer to read it.

"What's this?" I hissed and clicked back to try again.

"Don't bother," Rafe said as he came up behind me. "They won't grant you a pass yet. In fact, they aren't letting anyone have passes into or out of the Piper hub for a while."

"What do you mean?" I turned to study him.

"Three days ago, all travel permits in and out of the Pipes were blocked." Rafe dipped his head as he bent closer over a control board for a Z-rider. "They keep spouting about a contamination, but I have my theories."

"Theory?" I asked. I opened a link to Mia and started typing.

"Mia, I just discovered that I can't get a pass to come home right now. They are saying there's contamination. Are you ok? What is going on?"

I sent my message and turned back to Rafe. "Rafe, you said you had a theory."

Rafe didn't answer me, and I had to ask again before he looked my way. His face was dark, and his eyes didn't meet mine.

"Um, I'm pretty sure it's the Primers' response to the actions of our movement." He shrugged his shoulders.

"Response?" I turned back to my computer when Mia's reply beeped through.

"I'm fine. We are being told by the Forcers that the leak happened inside the connecting tunnel. They are telling us they should finish cleaning up before tomorrow. I have packed for you in case the repairs take longer."

Relieved that Mia was fine, I turned from the computer and studied Rafe. He looked guilty.

"Rafe, what have you done?" I moved over to stand in front of him.

"Well, you see..." He fiddled with a tool on the table between us until I slammed my hands down, then his eyes moved up to meet mine. "It was Breanna's idea, but Miles helped. We tagged the Prime's offices."

My blood went cold, and I had a fleeting image of the blue circle with a raised fist holding a pipe. "You put that symbol on the Primer's building?"

"We knew you wouldn't agree to it, so we didn't tell you." Rafe walked over to close the front door of the workshop, then turned back to face me. "Within hours after we tagged the office, the tube to your hub was locked down. Breanna warned me that her mother was raving to the Forcers' Master Commander that night and she—Deller, that is—insisted the Pipes hub be restricted until her Forcers could investigate."

"They shut down the connecting tunnel?" I asked, still not understanding what had happened. "Because of the symbol?"

Rafe nodded and walked back over to me, still refusing to meet my eyes. "They think someone from the Pipes has been spraying the symbol."

"They did this because of a sign?" I asked, thinking of all the Pipers, my people, who were trapped inside my hub, unable to get access to medical aid, printers, or anything else. It was true my hub was more independent than the others, but that didn't mean we didn't need medical help. Heck, not a day went by without a woman needing to go to the hospital for childbirth. And what would happen if there was an accident? Those people who weren't killed would need immediate medical aid.

The lies of a leak were transparent to me. The Pipers worked the tunnels, not the people in the Primer hub. Therefore, any "repairs" would have been done by Pipers, not the Forcers. Did others from my own hub know this explanation was a lie?

I worried more for Mia now that I understood the issue behind the lockdown. Turning, I saw Rafe shuffle his feet, waiting for my response to his actions. But it wasn't only him who had agreed to this—it was all of my friends. Friends who had been concerned and shocked to learn about my hub, a way of life they couldn't understand.

Why was it the Pipers were the only ones that didn't see the injustice of their lives? After all, a few kids painting a "demand for equality for the Pipers" sign resulted in the government locking my people in. It is restricting *our* lives, our chance for medical care and the right to move about our own world.

It was this last thought that had my blood turning hot. How was it a woman who sat in a high-rise in an entirely different hub could call the shots for my people? How was it that Primary Kasher had this kind of power?

When Rafe's eyes turned back to mine and saw that they were filled with anger about the injustice, he nodded once and slapped a hand on my right shoulder. "Welcome to the revolution. It's about damn time."

I was able to run home the day before school started. It took two hours for the Forcers to allow me into my own hub, and this angered me even further. But I kept my calm, knowing that my hub was now allowed access to medical care once again. I had to show the Forcers my student pass and travel orders, which the school had provided me with.

Mia had packed everything except my TWT, the two-way-talker I used to speak to Mitch.

Mitch still insisted we keep our friendship a secret, but since he was going to tutor me again this coming school year, I didn't worry as much if we were spotted talking to each other.

The night before I was expected at the Academy hub, my TWT emitted a loud squeak, and Mitch's small voice came out of the speaker.

"Zane, are you there?" Mitch asked.

I grabbed the device and turned it down, pulling the curtain of my room closed for some privacy.

"Yeah, I'm here," I replied.

"Zane, I heard there was no contamination." I nodded but gave no reply. "Zane, there's speculation about why we were locked in."

I knew what my friend would say, and part of me felt guilty on behalf of my other friends. The resistance was trying to get the other hubs to realize that the Pipers sacrificed everything so the other hubs could live a nice, safe life. Yes, they had restrictions within those cushiony lives, such as the one-child restriction. But their lives weren't put in danger every day when they went to work. Nor did they live in poorly built homes where their families fought for daily credits and food.

"What have you heard?" I asked. The knowledge of the resistance was fresh in my mind, but I was unwilling to tell Mitch. I knew where he would stand. He would insist on ending any actions against the government. He would think it was pointless and that these actions might result in danger.

"There's some noise about a band of troublemakers. Father says there were Forcers down in the tunnels asking about equality. Dad didn't understand, neither did the others," Mitch said, sighing. "I haven't told my family about this; I hope you haven't said anything either."

"I don't talk to your father," I said with a shake of my head.

"Zane, have you told Mia?" Mitch asked.

"She already knows. But I haven't told any other Pipers about this, Mitch," I said, feeling a little defensive now. But then I remembered *I* was the leading force behind the resistance, and my anger turned to guilt. "Mitch, they opened the tunnel back up. I'm sure it's just a glitch or something."

"Yeah, I guess. But Zane, please be careful who you talk to. Primary Kasher is once again picking me up. I think she finally believes me about not being in the tunnels the night that man was killed, but we still must be vigilant."

Mitch's warnings rang in my ears that night and kept me awake. When morning came, Mia was sad to see me off, but when Advisor Mathew Carlson, knocked on the door, I was ready with my bag and Z-rider.

"Ah, I am excited to say I got my little one the latest model of Z-rider," Mathew said with a smile as I climbed into the cart next to him. There was no driver, nor was the enrollment advisor, Tomson, with him this time, a fact

I was glad of, as Tomson always appeared to be judging me.

"Yes, I saw your name on the order list. I made sure to move your order ahead. I thought you were going to use it at the Academy," I said with a smile.

"Sadly, no. My wife is worried I would fall and break my neck. She thinks I have no coordination," he said with a laugh.

"We have Z-rollers. They have four wheels and are much safer for those who are..." I didn't know how to say older without offending him, but when he laughed and said, "Old" for me, I joined in his laughter.

"No offense taken. I know I'm old." He patted the steering wheel of the cart. "But I think my dear wife is correct. Even with four wheels I could do some damage."

Mathew dropped me off at the same dorm building I had been housed in last year. My new room was a floor higher this year. Miles was sitting in the cube closest to the door, and I saw Evan's chest plate and bags in the one across from him.

Knowing Rafe had been assigned the far-left cube, I set my stuff in the empty one and looked in the closet. New uniforms had been hung up, each now with the white level one triangle along the collar. My school tablet and supplies were stacked on the desk, each labeled with my initials.

"Rafe said he'll see us at dinner," Miles said as he stood in the opening to my cube. "Want to go play disc?" He held up the plastic toy.

"Sure."

Evan joined us an hour later, and when it got close to dinner, we headed over to the kitchen hall. I caught a glimpse of Mitch, who was eating at a table with two professors. We sat at the other end of the hall, and I wasn't surprised when Breanna and her friend Delany sat next to us a few minutes later.

"Delany has been helping me organize EFAP," Breanna said to me as she leaned closer. I could see she had grown taller. She had twisted her pretty hair up and put it in a knot on top of her head, so I could only guess about its current length. She smelled better than I remembered, and I felt the old shyness come back until I caught a glimpse of Miles, who was giving me a goofy grin.

"Eflap?" I asked.

"EFAP," she corrected. "Equality For All Pipers." She sat a bit taller. "Rafe got a message to me that you were with us now."

"Yeah," I said with a sober nod. "They shouldn't be able to block off my hub just because of some symbols," I grumbled, and when she gave me a smile, I felt my face heat up again.

"I agree." She cast a glance around the room. "Of course, we can't do much while we're at school, but Delany has an older cousin in the main hub who is keeping up the fight."

"Fight?" I asked, I heard the panic in my voice, so I tried again. "What fighting?"

"Well, there isn't any actual fighting." Breanna turned to study her meal. "I just mean he's spreading the word."

"He's been leaving pamphlets around at the local printers. Most of them are gone the next day, but we think the clerks are trashing some of them. I'm hopeful some people are reading them."

"How did your break go?" I asked her finally. I suddenly remembered she had to shadow her mother in the Primer offices for the two-month break.

"It was very insightful." She set her fork down. "It turns

out Mom doesn't make all the rules. There's a team. Well, it's more like a panel of advisors, and she leads this one. I only got to sit in on a few meetings, and I wasn't allowed in the meetings with the main committee, the one that Rafe's grandfather leads. But Mom's job is more restricted than I thought, at least more than they explained in government class."

My ears started buzzing when she mentioned Rafe's grandfather. Adam Waltson was a man I was very interested in.

"Rafe's grandfather went to a meeting with your mother?" I asked, hoping I sounded casual. I glanced quickly at Rafe, who sat a few seats down from us.

"Yeah, he's some head honcho," she provided with a shrug of her shoulders. "But I really didn't find out his job."

"Is he friends with your mom?" I asked.

She shook her head. "Actually, I think it's the opposite. Mom was furious after that meeting and stormed out of the room. Waltson, however, was smiling as if he'd won an argument."

Chapter 6

Education

I woke early the next morning and quickly got dressed. I opened my new schedule and saw I had some of the same classes as the previous year. Most were with the same teachers too. Some were named differently—instead of electronics it was now called technology, for instance. I had two new classes and smiled when I saw mechanics, which would be fun.

I frowned at the class titled accounting. I got along fine with math but didn't enjoy numbers as much as tinkering with my inventions. I waited until the others were dressed, then we headed down for breakfast.

I ate three helpings of flat cakes and two strips of protein flaps. Breanna barely touched her fruit orbs, and I smiled when she finally pushed her plate towards me.

"I don't think we have any classes together at all," she hissed with a pretty pout on her face.

"We have base class still," I said between mouthfuls of food.

"They moved my government class; I heard Mom discussing my schedule with the Head Dean last week."

She set her chin in her hands and rested her elbows on the table. "Mom doesn't want me in any of your classes."

"Do you blame her?" Evan asked as he devoured his large stack of flat cakes. "Z's a bad influence on you. After all, you did deck Weston last year." Breanna huffed once and shot Evan a nasty look. He just smiled mischievously then shoveled more food into his mouth.

"I have two classes with you," Miles interrupted with a sweet smile, which Breanna returned. Something deep down in my chest reared its ugly head, and I narrowed my eyes at Miles, who quickly bent back over his plate to eat.

I turned to her. She had her long hair tied back behind her ears today in a thick braid. She studied me, and the usual heat crept into my face. "We can eat lunch together and study afterwards. Plus, there's always dinner."

She pouted a little but nodded her head, then slowly smiled. "I guess."

Base class with Professor Luthier for the second level students was first. She had been our base class professor in the first year and would continue to be our professor until we finished our education. For some, this would be whatever level their parents deemed. For others, it would be until they no longer passed the tests. I hoped to obtain all ten levels.

I sat next to my bunk mates as we smiled and greeted several of our friends from the first year. Mitch was there, but I couldn't wave or acknowledge him. Breanna's friend Delany was back along with Rafe's girlfriend, Asher, who sat next to him.

Last to enter, right before the professor, was Weston and his two friends. Weston had grown another inch, and his usually short hair was now hanging over his ears. Manny, the usually giggly tall blond, came sulking in, followed by Omar, who I personally knew had a mean right hook.

All three looked mad, and neither of them even glanced my way, which was fine with me. After the previous year, I had reached my limit of conflict with them.

Professor Luthier started the class by stating all seats would now be assigned. We were all forced to gather our things and move about. Much to my dislike, I soon was sitting on one side of the room while my friends, including Breanna, were on the opposite.

I was just thinking about how long this year would be if I couldn't even sit with my friends when I saw Weston turn and flash a menacing smile my way. I narrowed my eyes at him then focused on the lesson.

Three classes later I knew the assigned seating wasn't normal policy. No other professors insisted on seating charts. This made me think Breanna's mother had demanded separation between her daughter and me. When lunch came, Breanna confirmed my speculation.

"I know she had something to do with this," Breanna said as she dropped next to me with a tray full of green orbs and fruit squares.

"Well, she is the Primer," Miles said as he joined us at our table.

"But this is ridiculous," Breanna murmured.

"Maybe she's worried Z will corrupt you," Rafe said with a wink, which caused me to blush.

"Speaking of..." Breanna said, and I turned my head to face her so fast that I heard something pop. "We need to have a meeting about you know what."

"Shh," Rafe said, casting a quick glance around. "Not here. I told you. Only after classes, and even then, only when we aren't near anyone."

"I know, but if the tagging stops, they will know it's being done by students," Breanna whispered.

"Shh. I told you I already have that figured out," Rafe replied with a stern look on his face. He refused to say anything more during lunch.

When lunch was finished, Breanna was still pouting as she went off for her government class while I went to my first mechanics glass with Professor Janson.

Evan had this class with me, and we walked across campus together to the oldest building in the hub. Old metal was painted to appear new, and the floors were made of cracked tile. Still, it was newer than anything in my hub and would have shamed all of the old and crumbling buildings in the Piper hub.

Professor Janson was a short messy man who wore overalls under his black robe. He had a thick lock of curly hair and narrow eyes that blinked too much, as if he had a hard time focusing on your face.

I was fascinated by the class. We spent much of the hour talking about ECHO's inner workings. Of course, nothing was said about the tunnels or the pipes. But the professor promised we would discuss elevators, building vents, and much more.

After this class I moved to my next lesson, accounting. I was discouraged when I saw Weston and Omar in the classroom, and I moved to sit as far from the two as I could. I was pleased when Mitch came in and sat right next to me.

"I was instructed to sit next to you in case you need tutoring with accounting as well," Mitch whispered with a smile.

My year looked a lot brighter, until Professor Linson came in. He was barely twenty and had thick brown hair and big brown eyes that studied the classroom. I swore I heard all the girls in the class sigh as their hearts fell on the floor at the man's feet.

I rolled my eyes and smiled at Mitch, who wrinkled his nose and shook his head in laughter.

My last lesson for the day was government class. In level one, I hadn't been interested in this course, but with my recent findings about Adam Waltson, I had a new interest in the way ECHO's government worked.

Rafe had the class with me, something I was both pleased and uncomfortable with. After all, it was his grandfather I was hoping to discover more about.

Rafe and I sat together as Professor Ricker came in. I knew from previous experience that she tended to drone on about the levels and layers of the government, but I needed to pay close attention. If Waltson was not in the government, like Rafe had stated, yet he attended several high meetings, then his job must be something provided within this lesson.

All levels, and all jobs, would be defined within the government class. We were given charts showing everything from the man who held the door open for the Primary to the woman in charge herself, Louise Kasher.

When the class was over, the details of Adam Waltson still eluded me, but I wasn't discouraged yet. I knew I wouldn't obtain the information overnight, because days of searching for Waltson and his job title had yielded nothing. Even Mitch, who loved to study and research, had yet to come across the details of Waltson's function.

We knew from my brief conversations with Rafe about his grandfather that he had a high-level job. We also knew from the Academy records that Waltson had a level of ten point five. Rafe's father too had held this level before he was murdered.

Since the Primary held a level of ten, and nothing in the records or registries indicated anything higher, Mitch and I were left with very little.

As we walked back to the dorm, we were met by Evan and Miles.

"We have ten new orders," Evan said with a smile as he pulled out his E-tablet and pulled up our page. "They are all from level one students who haven't had a chance to see a Z-rider in person, until today."

"This will put us further behind," Rafe stated with a shake of his head.

"Not if we hire out to build the riders while we're in school," I said suddenly.

"Hire out?" Miles asked as Evan laughed and clapped a hand on my back.

"That's the ticket!" Evan said with another laugh. "I know some young inventors, kids who can't afford the Academy. They can share the workshop with Dad, who could supervise them."

"Wait a minute," Rafe said with a frown. "Can we afford to hire anyone?"

"We can add it to the costs. I don't know if you three know, but sales have increased, which means we can increase the price," Miles provided. He had taken to keeping the books and running the accounting for the Z-riders, since the rest of us weren't interested in numbers.

"Maybe two or three hires can keep the riders in production while we are in school." Evan turned to Miles. "If we buy a business license today, we could get work started by the end of this week." The two soon had their heads bent closely as we walked back to start our homework. Evan thought hiring three technicians to build the Z-riders would do it, but Rafe seemed skeptical.

After schoolwork was completed and dinner consumed, we all met outside the dorm for some fun. Rafe had acquired a new disc that lit up when you threw it, which allowed us to play well after the dome's lights had dimmed.

We were having so much fun that it wasn't until a professor came and scolded us for being out too late that we noticed it was well past bed curfew. I had missed my scheduled talk with Mitch and was so tired that as soon as my head hit my pillow, I was out like the dome lights.

The dream which came to me was familiar.

The walls and pipes of the tunnels under my world were familiar. I felt comfortable as I roamed in the darkness of my dream.

Tunnels twisted and turned, and the soft buzzing of machinery was comforting me, until I turned a corner and saw the room where Hudson Adamson lay dead.

Sweat formed on my brow as I drew closer. I was unable to turn away from the gaping hole in his chest as his eyes looked up at me.

I knew this dream, the nightmare that had haunted me for over a year now. I knew what would come next and wanted to shake the fear from me but was unable to.

"You?" the man demanded. He coughed violently.

"She shot you!" I exclaimed, and the sound of the prior shot echoed in my ears. The sound bounced off the walls surrounding me and rang inside my head.

"Listen, find Waltson." The man gave another cough and grabbed my hand. "Find him, tell him, tell him I'm sorry." Another cough racked his body as he reached up and

gently ran a hand over my head. "I'm sorry," he said again, and this time I thought the apology was directed at me.

"Hold on, I can go get help," I urged as he gripped me harder.

"No, she controls them. Find Waltson," he repeated as he lowered his head. "You look like her." With this, he closed his eyes and took his last breath.

I awoke like I always did after these dreams, with tears in my eyes. My face was wet, and my heartbeat was erratic as my fears and feelings fought with the need to be quiet so my friends wouldn't discover my secret.

It took a while to calm down. The clock next to my bed told me I still had hours before I had to wake for school, but I knew sleep wouldn't come back to me this night.

I could still see Hudson's face in the dark and wondered for the first time if he had thought I was Rafe, his son. But that didn't feel right as his words came back to me again.

"You look like her." What had he meant by that? Who did I look like?

I thought about this for a while, then my mind returned to the echoing sound of the shot that had killed Hudson. I could hear it again, ringing in my mind, and my heart started to quicken.

I sat up quickly in bed when I realized it was the same sound, I had heard in the Fixer hub a few weeks ago. That night I had discovered the secret monitor room.

Someone had shot at me! I was sure of it now. So sure, that I glanced around the darkened room looking for the killer. When no one came out of the dark at me, I settled down.

Evan was snoring softly in his bunk, and the glow of the clock confirmed I was alone, safe inside my dorm room, surrounded by my friends.

I thought back to that dangerous night and realized I had been so exposed, walking alone in the Fixer hub all by myself. And that hadn't been the only time I had exposed myself. I had gone back several more times to the exact same location, alone, looking for entry into the secret room.

"Zap," I hissed at myself quietly in the darkness of my bunk. "I am such a fool."

Mitch had cautioned me that our friendship must remain a secret. His mother had exposed me as the possible witness to the murder. She had turned my name into our hub's advisor to collect a reward. It had only been Adam Waltson who had prevented any further speculation about my involvement. But that wouldn't stop the killer. Anyone who has killed surely wouldn't be stopped by an old man, despite his high-powered level.

But why had it taken the killer so long to attempt an attack on me? Maybe she had only recently learned of my involvement, or had doubts there had been a witness?

It didn't matter why it had taken so long. I felt—no, I knew—someone had shot at me. This meant the danger was now real, and I could no longer wander by myself after dark.

I had put myself in danger, and Mitch too, by leaving his map at the scene of the murder. If that was a shot at me in the Fixer hub, then both Mitch and I were in danger, and he had to be warned.

Chapter 7

Rules

I enjoyed school, despite the limitations and restrictions Breanna's mother had enforced. We still had meals together, and after school she and her friends would sometimes join us for disc. That is, until after the fifth day.

The day started normally. I got up and dressed. Rafe and Evan were teasing Miles about a girl who had spoken to him in the meal line at dinner the night before. We were just heading to breakfast when the APA system flared on. Head Dean Dickson's bald head flashed on the screen near the top of the dome as we students stopped to look up.

"I've never seen the dean," Evan said as he shook his head. "Man, he's as bald as a baby."

We all snickered until the dean started his announcement.

"Students of all levels, it is with great concern that I inform you that several facts have come to the attention of the administration office. To ensure these concerns are corrected, effective immediately there will be new rules and changes posted on the school site. The rules will be enforced by our newest staff member, Forcer Gunny Brackson. Forcer Brackson will have a small staff to ensure these rules and changes are implemented. Thank you and have a good day."

The message was brief, and with a shake of our heads, we continued on our way, not knowing our lives had just gotten a lot more complicated.

The first hint of trouble was when we sat in our assigned seats in base class. The professor insisted we pull up the rules and spend the first twenty minutes reading them.

Rules of the Academy

1. *No private carts of any kind will be used on campus.*
2. *No after-school activities not already authorized by the Head Dean will take place on campus.*
3. *All students must be in their dorm rooms before twenty hundred each evening.*
4. *Students will submit to a search of their dorm cubbies and/or person if a Forcer deems it is warranted.*
5. *Any student caught breaking rules is subject to disciplinary action.*

**Punishment will be approved by Head Dean Dickson.*

My heart was pounding in my ears long before I read rule five.

"This can't be right!" one student blurted out as I quickly scanned the rules again.

"How can they ban private carts?" another asked as Professor Luthier tried to bring some order to the classroom.

"Students!" she said, trying to cut through the barrage of questions. "Private carts have been banned due to a high number of injuries reported."

"I've only heard of one injury," one student said, pointing to where Miles was sitting. "And he's just fine now."

"Stutters a little though," another kid shouted, but there wasn't much laughter, as everyone who owned a Z-rider looked down towards their machines tucked under their chairs.

I glanced over to where my friends sat across the room, and my heart sank even more when I thought about how this would affect sales of our riders. Evan's face went pale as his dark eyes met mine. He shook his head once, but I saw Miles lift his chin a little in defiance.

After class he told us there was some good news. "The rules specifically said, 'on campus.'" He shrugged his shoulders. "At least we can still ride them on that side of the dome."

"But we use them to get to class," Rafe exclaimed, his deep voice raising a few pitches.

"We'll just have to take carts," Miles replied.

"If we can find any," Evan snorted as Rafe, and I headed off to technology class.

Two blocks away, Rafe and I were stopped by a thick-necked Forcer we had never seen before.

"Hold up, you two, just where do you think you're going?" the Forcer demanded.

"To class," Rafe said. He kept walking with me beside him. When the man blocked our path, we moved to pass him, but he held his thick arms out and grabbed Rafe's arm. "I think it's time for an inspection," he growled. He started to pull Rafe's bag off his shoulder.

"Who are you?" Rafe demanded, gripping his bag tighter.

"I'm a Forcer," the brute growled just as a loud ripping noise emanated from the bag.

"Hey! That was a gift!" Rafe said as he released his hold on the bag.

Rafe's bag hit the ground, and several books and his school tablet hit the floor. A loud snap and sizzle could be heard from the machine as the man turned to reach for my bag.

"You're going to pay for that!" Rafe said as he bent to retrieve the broken machine just as I handed my bag to the man.

"You didn't submit to the search; it's your fault, and I'm not paying for anything." The Forcer pulled all of my books and my tablet out and threw them to the floor.

I had tried to prevent the broken bag and tablet by handing the Forcer my possessions. However, when my tablet sat on the sidewalk sizzling next to Rafe's broken one, I narrowed my eyes and studied the man's name tag.

"Forcer Woodson, we will be lodging a formal complaint and request for reimbursement of these tablets and his bag," I said as I too bent down to retrieve my books.

"Do what you want," the man replied. As he turned to leave, his left foot sent my tablet skipping along the sidewalk.

"He can't do that!" Rafe growled as he held his broken tablet up between two of his fingers. The popping and sparks had stopped, but pieces of the screen fell out and onto the ground.

"Do we have time now to run to the dean's office?" I asked.

"No, we will have to go after third period," Rafe said as he shoved the broken tablet into his ripped bag.

"And miss lunch?" I asked. My voice had the same whiny tone Rafe had used only minutes before.

Rafe and I met at the kitchen hall before heading to the dean's office. We couldn't use our Z-riders and couldn't find any available E-carts, so we started walking. The walk took longer than I remember.

When we walked into the building, I knew we wouldn't have time for lunch. The entryway was full of students and even a few professors.

"I don't care whose orders they are following; they confiscated my rider and wouldn't believe I was a professor even after I showed them my halo badge." At the sound of Professor Lindson's voice, the hush grew inside the entryway. All eyes turned to where the dean stood behind his assistant.

"Professor Lindson, as I told you before, I am sorry the Forcers took your machine. It will be returned once we have worked out the kinks in these new rules," Dean Dickson advised, and I saw a line of sweat roll down his bald forehead and disappear into his thick beard.

"But what about me?" a student who had a green triangle on his collar shouted. "They broke mine. Who's going to pay for that!"

"And they smashed my E-pod, which was a gift from my father," a tall girl with long black hair shouted while holding up a still-smoking orb.

"We will take all of your complaints. Just fill out the form that Sarah will send you, then we can work things out." The dean made waving motions with his hands.

"How long will that take?" Rafe said, holding up his broken tablet. "They broke our school tablets, and we need them for our work."

At this, Professor Lindson waved us forward. "They smashed school equipment?" His brown eyes looked at us as both Rafe and I nodded our heads.

"And ruined my pack," Rafe added, holding up his bag.

"Head Dean," Professor Lindson said, turning his eyes to where the dean stood, "I can wait, but these students need their tablets replaced now. Is there anyone else with broken school equipment caused by these new Forcers?"

Three more students came forward, and Sarah collected the broken tablets. The dean didn't utter a word.

"Here, follow me, and I will move your data over to new tablets," Sarah said as she opened a cabinet behind her desk.

While we were getting our data transferred to our new tablets, the room continued to fill behind us. One more broken tablet was added to Sarah's pile, and a tiny older professor joined in the complaints. Forcers had interrupted her third period class, insisting they be allowed to search students for Z-riders in her classroom.

"Z, it kind of sounds like they are targeting people with our riders," Rafe whispered to me.

Rafe didn't have to tell me this. I had already come to this conclusion. I also knew who was behind these new Academy rules.

"I need to talk to Breanna," I replied as Professor Lindson came up to us.

"Boys, it appears there are a lot of broken Z-riders, mine included. They will all require repairs. Do you think your company will be able to perform them?" The professor looked at us imploringly.

Rafe looked at the Head Dean, and I was completely shocked by his reply. "We can do the repairs. But we feel any damage done by the Forcers should be paid out of their budget."

"I second that request," said Professor Lindson and several students.

The dean wouldn't approve anything until all complaints were collected and a review was done. Even then he said he would have to talk to his financial advisor. He promised he would start the reviews right away and asked that everyone fill out the complaint forms before they left.

I never did get lunch that day. My stomach grumbled all through mechanics, and by the time I got to accounting I thought I would faint from hunger.

When Professor Lindson passed my desk and placed a protein bar in front of me, I smiled at him and he gave me a wink.

"What is that about?" Mitch asked as he sat next to me.

"We have a mutual enemy," I replied as I took a huge bite out of the bar.

"What?" Mitch asked as Weston and Omar passed by our desks, laughing.

"I heard Dad is whipping this campus into shape," Omar pronounced as his eyes landed on me.

"It's about time," Weston said loudly. "Too much riffraff if you ask me. This school now allows Pipers, can you believe that?"

"Boys!" Professor Lindson scolded. "Take your seats."

"Who is Omar's dad?" I wondered, taking another bite of my bar.

When Mitch sighed, I looked over and saw him shake

his head at me. "Forcer Gunny Brackson, the new head Forcer for the Academy."

"What?" My amazed statement was a little too loud, and the professor sent me a stern look, but he didn't scold me as he started his lesson.

At dinner that night, I finally had a chance to talk with Breanna. She looked pale and only had two slices of wheat cakes on her plate when she sat next to me.

"Z, we have trouble coming," she hissed, looking about the room quickly.

"I know. These new Forcers are making a big mess of everything." I moved some of my protein rounds onto her plate. "Do you know if your mom is behind all of this?"

"That's just it." Breanna flinched. Her action caused me to quickly look up as two large men entered the kitchen hall. "It's not Mom. In fact, I know for sure that Mom is furious. She sent me a warning message just after breakfast. She wants me to stay away from the Forcers and told me to never walk alone. She said she was worried they were here to get me kicked out of school."

"What?" I turned my eyes away from the two Forcers to Breanna's brown eyes. "Get you kicked out? Why?"

"There are some in the government who wish that my family would be taken out of the Primer's office. Some of them have been trying to take over for years."

"But they can't do that." I looked over to where Rafe sat listening. "Can they?"

"I don't know." Rafe shook his head. "But I know these Forcers can't get you kicked out of school."

"How do you know?" Breanna asked, pushing her plate away.

"Because Weston and his goons tried to get Z kicked out last year and it didn't work," Rafe replied with a smile.

"But that was different," Breanna insisted.

"No, it wasn't. Just like you, someone is paying for his education, and the school won't kick a student out on the word of another student. Only when laws are broken, or levels aren't passed, is a student not allowed to return. My grandpa told me this last year." Rafe patted Breanna's hand once, then turned to look over his shoulder at the Forcers, who were walking around the room, looking menacing.

"All they can do is write a request for disciplinary action. They can't even write tickets," Mitch said as he walked over to sit at our table.

Seeing Mitch boldly walk up and sit next to me had my eyes going wide. "I need to schedule our tutoring classes," he said quickly. He lowered his brows as if scolding me for appearing shocked.

"How do you know that?" Breanna asked Mitch.

"I asked Professor Luthier after base class this morning. Two of the Forcers tried to take my Z-roller in front of the Professor. You should have heard her scold the two men. I thought they were going to pee their pants when she got done with them," Mitch said with a laugh.

"Are you sure they can't have me kicked out of school?" Breanna asked, turning her eyes back towards the two men who had taken up post next to the doors of the room.

"Positive," Mitch replied, then he turned to me. "Will you need any assistance with any other classes this year?" he asked.

"Um." Our sessions allowed us face-to-face time, time alone to speak. If I said I didn't need any help, then that would stop. "I think I'm going to need help with accounting."

Mitch nodded then stood and smiled down at Breanna. "Don't worry about the Forcers. Professor Luthier thinks they won't be here long." Then he turned to me. "Tuesdays and Thursdays, the time changed to sixteen hundred. Oh, I have a few more students so we will be a little more crowded than last year." With this, Mitch hobbled away.

Breanna sighed once, then grabbed my plate and started to eat all of my protein and rice cakes with a new vigor.

Chapter 8

Terrors

With dinner ending earlier and the new curfew, the new rules were very restricting. There weren't going to be any more games of disc in the open space in front of our building, nor goofing off on our Z-riders. In fact, there wouldn't be any more riders for us during our time at the Academy.

We knew the Forcers were even trying to take the professors' riders from them. We found this funny until Miles pointed out that we'd had ten orders cancelled by professors and twenty-four from students.

"What are we supposed to do with our time?" Evan complained as he tried to bounce an ugly purple ball around in the small space between his cot and Rafe's desk.

"I guess we can move our study time to right after dinner," I suggested. I frowned when I realized my Tuesdays and Thursdays would be filled with nothing but studying.

"OK, then what?" Evan replied. "We can't zip on our riders. We can't have any activities either."

"I have already submitted a request to toss the disc

around, but I had to call it a sport and request permission to start a team." Rafe shook his head as he caught Evan's purple bouncy ball and threw it at his head.

"Did they say how long before you get approval?" I asked. I had to stop my foot from twitching as I leaned against the wall.

"Don't know. It might take longer than we were told to get my bag replaced," he replied with a frown. "Mom said she's going to lodge a complaint with the Master Commander. She went to school with her, and they have remained friendly." Rafe ducked when Evan threw the ball at his head in return.

"The Master Forcer's a girl?" Evan asked, shock on his face as he caught the ball Rafe had thrown at him.

We had a quick game of ball, but it mostly consisted of us trying to hit each other in the face, then laughing whenever someone didn't duck quickly enough. When bedtime finally came, I grabbed my TWT and excused myself to the bathroom.

"Zane!" Mitch's voice was quiet, and there was a lot of static on the machine. I fiddled with the levers, trying to get a better reception.

"Hey, Mitch," I said, but Mitch replied quickly before I could say anything more.

"Listen, destroy your TWT, do it now! Take it apart so no one can tell what it is. I'll try and tell you more tomorrow. But do it immediately!"

With this, the machine went dead in my hands. I knew Mitch wouldn't panic unless there was a reason, so before I left the bathroom, I had half the TWT taken apart. When I returned to my desk, I finished the job. The parts lay in a small pile when I went to bed that night.

I was worried but didn't speak about it to the others.

Instead, I lay awake for a while pondering what had Mitch worried about our TWTs. Why would he be worried about my machine but not his? Had someone discovered his, and he was worried they could trace it back to me?

There were so many questions spinning around in my head that it was two hours before I was finally able to fall asleep. I was soundly sleeping when, two hours later, the lights blasted on, and voices started shouting. I was so tired and confused that all I could do was lie there in bewilderment.

"Out, you little zits," a deep voice blasted, and I was rudely shaken awake and roughly pulled from my cot.

As my body flew through the air, I had a fleeting hope that this dream wouldn't end with the dead man down in the Pipe tunnels again. But when my head and left shoulder hit the wall hard, I realized I was awake, and this wasn't a dream.

"Hey!" a voice shouted, and our dorm advisor Tyler came barging in and stood over me, his skinny body stiff and his bony fists raised. "Don't lay your hands on the students!"

"Out of my way," came a growl, but Tyler stood his ground.

"The rule says we must submit to searches. It doesn't give you the right to abuse students!" Taylor shouted, thumping a fist on his own chest. "I'm studying to be a legal advisor for my grandfather's firm, and if you lay another hand on any student inside this building, you will have an action filed against you before zero six hundred, Mr. Brackson!"

By the time the ringing in my ears stopped, I had been assisted up off the floor by Tyler and Miles and escorted out into the hallway.

"Do you need a doctor?" Miles asked as I stood rubbing my shoulder and shaking my head to clear it.

"What?" I looked at Tyler, and when I saw two of him, I turned and looked at Rafe, who stood at the door to our room. He appeared to be swaying, then he split into two images. Loud crashing noises could be heard from beyond.

"If they break anything..." Rafe hissed and turned to Tyler.

"Don't worry, this was a scheduled search." The dorm advisor frowned as he looked at me. "Though they shouldn't be throwing anyone around." I wasn't sure if there were two Tylers or just one, but both shook their heads at me and moved over to Rafe. "I'm going to call a nurse just in case. He looks a little green right now."

Miles helped me sit down in the hallway and when I blinked again, the nurse was standing over me.

"Did he lose consciousness?" I heard her ask. When Miles replied, his words seemed strange to me. A bright light flashed in my eyes, and my head immediately began pounding.

"I'll call a doctor," she responded quickly.

"Call my mom. I think she will want to be here anyway," Miles insisted as a loud crash sounded from inside our room.

"Can you imagine, waking up students at this hour and then tossing them into the wall," the nurse clucked as she moved off.

I blinked again and this time a man was leaning over me. He had a high forehead, a thick shaggy mustache over his top lip, and kind brown eyes similar to his son's. The hated light was there again, and I heard him talking in a deep voice to someone over his shoulder. "Just hold still. It looks like you have a concussion," he said with a frown.

"Shelly, love, hand me that neck brace. Then I'll see about waking the dean."

My neck was pinched as a brace was wrapped around my neck, and I was given a shot before the man moved out of my limited line of sight. Then Miles's mother was there. Her lips were set in a frown as she put a blanket over me. "That was Miles's father, Doctor Scottson. You haven't met him yet. He wouldn't let me come alone tonight." She looked over her shoulder. "And it was a good thing too."

She didn't expand on this, but Miles shoved into my vision and studied me. "His pupils are they supposed to be that way?" he asked his mom. His words made my worry that my face was somehow deformed now.

"Shh. You'll frighten him," she scolded. But she answered him, her tone taking on that of a teacher. "That happens when there is swelling in the brain. Did you see how he reacted to the light?" She leaned forward to take my pulse. "His pulse is erratic too. Here, feel."

When Miles lifted my left hand, I cried out in pain.

"Oh no," Doctor Sanderson said, pushing her son away. "Oh, your shoulder is dislocated. Shelly, better call for a stretcher." She turned away, then came back with another shot, her face filled with concern and a little anger. "We will get you all fixed up. Sleep now."

My world went dark.

The pain woke me, and I saw the familiar hospital walls and smelled the clean sterile air. When I heard Evan's low grumble, I tried to lift my head to see who was near me.

"I wouldn't try that if I were you," Rafe said, but I didn't need to be told twice, as the pain in my neck almost caused me to black out again.

"What, who," I croaked out. I heard Evan snicker once before Miles quieted him with a harsh "Shhh."

"Z, my man, you have been on quite an adventure," Rafe said as he came into view. He was still in his pajamas. His dark hair was ruffled but his eyes glinted with excitement.

"Tell him about the dean," Evan insisted, and Rafe glanced at him. He nodded once as he turned back to me.

"All in good time. First, how do you feel?" Rafe studied me with his brown eyes.

"Light," I replied, and Rafe smiled.

"Good. Miles's mom said as long as you didn't move too much the medication would help with the pain. Okay, first, you missed a lot."

"Hurry, Mom or Dad might be back soon," I heard Miles insist, but I still only saw Rafe standing over my bed.

"Yeah, yeah," Rafe said impatiently as he waved his hands towards the other side of my bed. "I will if you two would stop interrupting me. Well, after you fainted, the Head Dean showed up. Apparently, Tyler called his girlfriend. You know Sarah who works in the Head Dean's office, right?" He didn't wait for a reply but continued. "Anyway, he told Sarah about the attack, and she insisted that the dean should know right away. So, she called him home, and he rushed over and got to our dorm even before the stretcher came. He was livid and stormed into our room while the Forcers were still conducting the search. For what, I still don't know. They made a right mess of our stuff, broke your Z-rider and Miles's mechanic projects that he had already finished. They kept stating it was a bomb or something."

"Luckily, we don't keep any revolution stuff on us," I heard Miles's mumble, but Rafe continued as if he hadn't heard him.

"So, Head Dean starts yelling about how he is going to call Joan and that Forcer Brackson and his men were going to be banished from the Academy. He was angry, and his little bald head was redder than your left eye." With this I winced a little, but he continued. "The dean said he wasn't going to be blackmailed into continuing with the agreement, and that they had cost more in one day than the Academy made from the tuition of one student an entire year."

"Tell him about the—" Evan's began, but Rafe shushed him again.

"As they were loading you up on the stretcher, more Forcers came, but these were from the main hub. Doctor Scottson, Miles's dad, he called the main hub and sent for them. It appears they were sent so they could arrest the other Forcers. See, they aren't allowed to harm students, no matter what. And man, throwing you from your bed while you were still asleep is against the rules or something."

"You should have seen Omar's dad. He was pissed," Evan said from somewhere in the room.

"Yeah, well, they didn't arrest him or the others, but they were sent back to the main hub and, dude, you have to get better because they are setting a trial. We all have to go, even Tyler, because he saw the whole thing." Rafe looked down at me with a reassuring smile. "When you're better, that is."

"Here they come!" Miles hissed, and I could hear the thumping of Mia's shoes as she rushed into my room.

"Oh my!" Mia exclaimed, and then I saw her concerned face over me. She looked older, and her hair wasn't in her usual neatly combed bob. She still wore her night dress, with one of her shawls over her shoulders. "What have they done to you?"

I tried to give her a reassuring smile and realized my left front tooth was missing. I ran my tongue in the empty slot and tasted blood.

"Oh, yeah, they had to pull that," Rafe said as he studied me again. "But the doctors said it can be replaced later after the swelling goes down."

Miles's mother had come in with Mia, and she told her about my injuries. I heard words like *concussion*, *torn rotator cuff*, and *limited motion*. I also heard about the missing tooth and swollen eye, which explained why I could only see out of my right eye.

Mia was told I would stay for twenty-four hours for observation and then could return to school in a limited capacity. Doctor Sanderson said she would forward these instructions to my professors and was just leaving when the Head Dean walked into my room. He leaned over me to study my face.

"Such a shame. I am so sorry this happened," Head Dean Dickson said with a shake of his head as he turned to look at Mia. "Rest assured, my dear woman, that the men responsible for this will be held accountable. I already have the Academy's legal team working on setting the trial date. These men will pay for their crimes against your ward."

"Thank you, Dean," Mia said as she tucked the sheet tighter around me. "Would you be kind enough to tell my friend in the hallway that I will contact him later today," Mia said in way of a dismissal. It was successful, because Dean Dickson nodded once and then left. I didn't know who Mia's friend was, but I saw her turn and frown at my bunk friends. "You three might as well go on back to your dorm. I think your friend Tyler got most of the bunks back together except for one, which the brutes tore the stuffing out of."

Each of my friends came over and told me to get better soon, then they too left. Mia made a big production of inspecting my left arm, which was strapped close to my chest. The pain was numbed by drugs and only my head hurt, but since the lights were low, my discomfort was minimal.

"There, now that the shot wore off, it appears we must keep you awake," Mia said as she sat on the edge of my bed. Her smile was warm, but I saw worry in her eyes.

"What friend?" I asked. My words felt funny without a front tooth. Mia frowned once, then straightened her shoulders.

"Well, if you must know, I've been seeing Forcer Carrington," she explained, but my confusion increased. "You remember him. He came to our rescue when we were in the Primer hub."

"I know." I frowned until my lips hurt. "Why?"

"Why what, dear?" Mia asked.

"Why didn't you tell me earlier." I tried to give her a smile.

Chapter 9

Impacts

The Academy was all abuzz when I returned to my dorm the next morning. Mia helped me back to my room along with the Head Dean, who drove the E-cart himself.

When I saw several students riding Z-riders, I asked about it. I was told the rules had been halted until further notice. It appeared there were too many complaints from parents and faculty members.

"And with the recent development, let's just say the Forcers are no longer enforcing on campus, unless called directly by me," Head Dean explained with a frown on his face.

The dorm room had been cleaned, and I noticed my mattress was new and Miles had a new school tablet. My Z-rider was missing and so were the parts to my dismantled TWT. Some of my clothes were being laundered, according to Rafe, who explained that they had been thrown on the ground and stomped on.

"They should come back later this evening, before school tomorrow," Rafe explained.

Once I was settled in, Mia returned to the Pipe hub and the dean disappeared, leaving me alone with my friends.

"Don't forget, you have a lighter load for several weeks while you recover," Miles instructed as he handed me a sheet of paper. "Mom says you aren't to use your tablet until she says so. Electronics can be harmful during this time. Last year when I had my concussion, it took three weeks before I could even look at my tablet." Miles was speaking of when we snuck down into the Pipe tunnels. We had been chased by the Forcers, and he had bumped his head on the ladder rungs leading out of the tunnels. Of course, we had told everyone that Miles had fallen off his Z-rider.

"How am I supposed to do my schoolwork?" I asked. I cleared my throat when I heard the whiny sound coming out of it.

"That has been taken care of," Rafe said with a wink. "You know that kid Mitch? Well, the dean asked him to help you during this time, which means you won't fall too far behind."

I was ecstatic about this news. If Mitch was assigned to help me, then we would see a lot of each other.

When we went to dinner that night, I was surrounded by classmates before I could get in line for food. Everyone wanted to hear about my fierce battle with the Forcers. Some were disappointed when I told them I didn't remember much, while others still wanted to hear about everything.

Breanna helped me with my tray and made sure all my favorite foods were piled on, while the others kept telling their version of events.

"You should have seen Tyler standing there, blocking Z from Forcer Gunny," Evan said for the third time that evening.

"He stood up to them," I confirmed, still amazed by our dorm advisor's actions.

"I heard he spat at one," a first level student insisted.

"I heard he got punched too," a fifth level said, but Rafe shook his head.

"Nah, he just threatened them with legal action," Rafe said to everyone's laughter.

When the crowd dispersed and I could finally eat my meal, which I was finding difficult, as my replacement tooth hadn't been installed yet, Evan poked me in the ribs on my good side.

"Doesn't look like Omar and Weston are happy tonight,' Evan said as he pointed towards the other end of the room with a large disc of bread.

Weston and Omar were sitting, and Manny was standing behind them. All three were glaring in my direction. I didn't care. After all, it was Omar's dad that had injured me two nights before. Instead, I turned back to my plate and smiled when Breanna started cutting my fruit orbs into smaller sizes.

"So, you can eat them. At least until your tooth is replaced," she said with a sly smile.

"I don't know, Z, I think it's an improvement on your face," Evan said with a laugh.

"Nah, we can't have him too roughed up." Rafe studied me with a serious expression on his face. "Although, it makes you look older."

My evening was complete when Mitch walked over to our table using his crutch. I saw he had grown and took note that I would have to adjust his crutches at a later time so he wouldn't have to bend so much.

"I'm glad you're feeling better," Mitch said in a shy voice as he studied me. "I think you're allowed to attend classes, and the dean adjusted my schedule so I can sit next to you and take notes. But I'm not taking programing, so maybe one of your friends can take your notes for you?"

"I can help." Miles spoke up.

"Sure, that would be great," Mitch replied. He was turning to leave when Head Dean walked into the room and came over to us. Mitch stopped and remained standing at our table, then nodded his head at the dean.

"Good, good, you are all here. Oh, hello, Mitch, I assume you have scheduled everything with Zane, that's good." When the dean waved a hand at Mitch, my friend nodded and quickly moved away. "Well, I have just received word that the trial is set for four days from now. The school lawyers wish to speak to you all, and I took the liberty of scheduling a meeting with them for tomorrow, while the incident is still fresh in your minds." He gave each of us a weak smile and turned when he saw Breanna sitting next to me. "Oh, Ms. Bryer, I didn't see you there," the dean said.

"Hello, Dean," Breanna said, then she quickly excused herself. I was shocked by her quick departure but turned back to the dean when he continued talking.

"Mr. Hudson, the lawyer's office is two buildings down from your mother's office in the main hub. I took the liberty of getting passes for tomorrow and will drive you myself. I think we can all fit into one cart. I can pick you up at zero eight hundred tomorrow. I think school uniforms will suit everyone at this time, but I have had your parents send more formal clothing for the court date. Except you, Zane. Financial Advisor Mathew is working on your court outfit." When he was done talking, he nodded once then turned and left us, his chubby legs did a quick step through the sea of students. Most were openly gaping at the dean's presence in the kitchen hall.

When he had been gone several minutes, Breanna came back and sat down next to me.

"Sorry about that." She looked around the room. "Mom insisted that the dean keep me from hanging out with you."

"I can't imagine why?" Rafe smirked as he started eating again.

I slept fitfully that night. My head hurt, and I kept imagining the sound of boots in the hallway, no doubt Forcers coming to get me. When the alarm went off, I had a migraine, and Miles had to fetch my medicine. However, I couldn't take it on an empty stomach, so we went for break-fast quickly before meeting the dean back at our dorm.

When he arrived, he was with the school enrollment advisor, Vince Tomson. They were each driving a cart because Tyler had been asked to join us too.

"Oh, good, you are all here," Head Dean said with a grim expression. "Change of plans. Our meeting is now at the courthouse. I am being told it's just an informal meeting with the judge, but security has increased due to recent circumstances."

Confused by this statement and change, I turned to look questionably at Rafe, who shrugged his shoulders as we climbed into one of the carts.

Since neither the dean nor Advisor Vince offered any further explanations, we rode to the tunnel in silence. The number of Forcers guarding the tunnel had increased since my last visit out of the hub. They questioned the Head Dean, and even when they handed in the forms and passes, wanted to know why students were leaving on a school day.

We saw the dean's face turn bright red as he slowly explained the meeting. Another ten minutes passed before the Forcers would let us through. I could hear the dean mutter under his breath. All I could make out was "her fault" and "disrespectful," but seeing the dean agitated had my anxiety increasing.

The Primer hub seemed different to me this trip. There were fewer people walking along the streets, and those who were out seemed to be in a hurry. I saw a mother dragging her child down the street, and when she spotted us, she quickly ducked into the nearest door. I quickly looked around, not knowing what I expected to see, but when I saw nothing, I turned to Rafe, who once again shook his head and shrugged.

Tensions were high as we drove further into the heart of the hub. The tall buildings were impressive. The white of the walls contrasted with the shine of the glass, and the green of plants seemed almost fake. It wasn't until we turned the last corner that my confusion and tension turned to full-blown fear.

The courthouse was an impressive five-story building sitting amongst the high towers. Two large pillars sat on the steps, as if they were sentinels guarding the entryway. No windows or glass adorned the front, only cold white stone blocks. I had a fleeting thought of prison when I looked at the building. Yet it wasn't the building that caused the panic in me, it was the people.

There were thousands of people covering the steps into the courthouse and blocking the street. Some held up E-pods, others had signs, and they were all shouting.

There seemed to be two different groups. One had dark red signs with black slashes on them. The people holding these seemed to be shouting the loudest. "Pipers stay home!" some shouted while others chanted, "For Forcers!"

The other group had signs portraying the familiar raised fist surrounded by a blue circle. Their chants were almost drowned out, but a clear "Equality for all" was heard through the drum of the other voices.

"Oh, zap," Rafe said, placing one of his hands on my arm. "Stay low."

"I was afraid of this," the dean said, quickly turning the wheel. Our cart raced down the closest alleyway. I saw Vince turn the second cart with Tyler and Evan clinging to the handholds. Both quickly looked over their shoulders back at the crowd.

"Dean, what is going on?" Rafe asked as we drove down another block and turned right, back towards the center of the hub.

"It appears this incident has caused a political debate. There is a new faction demanding equality for the Pipes, and they have recently become more, how should I put it, vocal." The dean wiped sweat from his brow. "Once word of the incident got out, well, let's just say politics got involved. Some say this was caused by having our first Piper students at the Academy." Here the dean turned and looked at me with sober eyes. "I want you to know I have been quite vocal that this is not the case. You and Mr. Frankson have been exemplary students."

I gave a weak smile to the dean as he continued.

"This EFAP group has been trying to blast the politicians for equality. Their group has grown quite a bit in the last few days," he finished as we pulled up to the back wall of the courthouse.

We all climbed out of the carts as the Head Dean

moved to the single door and knocked quickly. To my shock, it was opened by Rafe's grandfather, Adam Waltson.

"Quickly, is this everyone?" Adam asked, his face set with a frown as he moved to hug Rafe. "I'm glad you made it safely. The meeting is about to start. I had to stall them by saying I needed to use the bathroom. But they can't really start without me," Adam said as his tan eyes turned to study me. I swear I saw him wink and send a reassuring smile my way.

Adam wasn't dressed as a Piper this time, nor a Fixer. Instead, he was dressed in a dark suit. There was a wink of gold at his wrists and on the cloth hanging from around his neck. Over the dark suit he wore a black robe. It had triangles of all the levels embroidered down the opening. The zipper hung open.

"Quickly, head down this hallway and up the stairs to room 407. I will be along shortly." He didn't wait for our reply but released Rafe and headed in the opposite direction. His pace quickened as the dean grabbed my arm gently and ushered us in the opposite direction.

"Now remember, just tell the truth, and you all will have nothing to fear," the Head Dean urged, but I swore I heard fear in his voice. "If you can't answer a question, let our lawyers handle it."

"Who are our lawyers?" Evan asked, his voice filled with fear.

"Oh, I'll introduce you once we get there," the dean said as we stepped out into a large foyer. I had seen several buildings since being in the Academy hub, but nothing had prepared me for this entryway.

Marble walls, marble floors, and a marble ceiling gave the open room a warm glow. Hidden lights and ornate sconces lit the room with golden colors. There were a few people loitering around the base of a grand staircase. The men were dressed in suits while the woman wore pretty colorful dresses and heels.

I must have stopped because when the dean tugged on my arm, I almost lost my balance.

"Hurry, my boy," he said as Rafe and my friends moved to stand around me. I didn't know why until after the first flash. Then the shouting of questions bombarded me, and I finally understood that the people were all reporters.

There weren't many news stations in ECHO, only two in fact. But each station employed over fifty people fighting to get the exclusive story, and it seemed they were all here in the courthouse's foyer.

"Mr. Noman is it true you attacked the Forcers when they tried to complete a search of your quarters?" one woman shouted while another asked if I was the head behind the Piper equality group.

"Is it true the Forcers found EFAP paraphernalia in your dorm?" another reporter shouted as we made our way past them to the stairs.

This type of questioning had my steps faltering again, but luckily the dean still had a grip on my arm. He pushed me forward while the flashes from halo cameras continued to blind me.

I didn't know what to do. My face was still bruised and battered from the beating I had taken only two days before. The flashes didn't help my concussion, and my eyes hurt whenever a halo was taken of me. I closed my eyes briefly and almost missed the first step. Luckily Rafe was there. He grabbed my other arm and helped the dean as they carried me up the marble steps and away from the reporters.

Chapter 10

Meeting

The reporters must not have been allowed up beyond the foyer because, as we rounded the steps to another landing, the flashing lights stopped. It didn't help the headache which had formed behind my eyeballs. For each of my heartbeats, I felt a solid pounding inside my skull.

Occasionally I could hear talking from below, but as we climbed higher into the building, the chaos was left behind us, or so I thought. When we got to room 407, there were others waiting outside the door leading into the room. I took a deep breath of relief when Head Dean smiled and rushed forward to meet the two men.

"Ah, Fitz and James," Head Dean Dickson said as he shook hands with both men. Fitz was a tall skinny man with a wave of black hair on his head. He looked odd because the hair on the side of his head was white. But his eyes looked kind as he slapped a hand on the dean's shoulder. James was the same age as the dean. He had a thinning head of bright red hair and a thick mustache.

"Dick, it appears our meeting has turned into a full

production," James stated as he shook his head. "Let's meet these clients first and see if we can get this over and done with."

Introductions were given, and the lawyers shook everyone's hands, including mine. I pushed through the pain and gave each man a weak smile. Shortly after the introductions, the door to room 407 opened and the Primary's advisor, Davis Elliotson, cleared his throat.

"Oh, you have finally arrived. Very well, please make your way into the room." Elliotson's young face was set firmly in a frown as he looked down at each of us boys as we filed into the room.

We entered the small chamber. It was no bigger than the dean's office, but it was packed with people. I saw the white head of Adam sitting at the end of a table. I also noted the blonde head of Primary Kasher sitting next to him. She too wore a black robe, and her neat short hair was pinned back away from her face, giving her a stern look.

There were twelve men and women sitting at a rectangular table that filled the room. Fitz and James led us to the table's left end. When I glanced to my right, there were several large men and a small woman sitting along the other side of the table. At first it was the men I focused on; each had the build of a Forcer. One man was Gunny Brackson. I only knew him from the picture Miles had shown me after my injuries.

When I was done studying each, I focused on the woman and was shocked to discover she was the same dark-haired girl from the Printer hub, the one who had hassled me before school had started. She sat next to the Forcers as if she belonged, a frown on her face as she returned my gaze. She no longer wore the ill-fitting jumpsuit but an expensive red shirt with a black skirt. Her long hair was twisted up similar to a bun Breanna had worn once. Spiked thin heels tapped the floor as she boldly studied me with her dark eyes.

My injured mind tried to formulate a reason why she was there, or who she was, but the pounding in my head seemed to beat faster the more I thought. My mouth hung open with shock, and it wasn't until Evan elbowed me that I realized I had missed the introduction into the proceedings.

"This meeting is to establish whether or not a formal hearing will take place in three days' time," Primary Kasher said as she studied a tablet sitting in front of her. "It is my understanding that the Forcers, both Gunny Brackson and Simon Woodson, were the cause of the incident." When the dark-haired woman sitting with the Forcers stood, Primary Kasher paused. After glancing at the dark-haired woman with a frown on her face, she cleared her throat and said sternly, "Master Commander, I have not finished the overview yet. You will have time to debate afterwards."

"If you please, it is our wish to dispense with this meeting so we can file our own charges," the Master Commander replied.

"Charges?" Adam asked, one brow lifted as he studied the woman. "What charges and against whom?"

The woman addressed as Master Commander turned and, without blinking, looked right at me. "Against Zane Noman for refusal to follow rule number four in the new rules of the Academy. He refused to submit to a peaceful search of his dorm cubby."

My mouth must have dropped open again because Evan elbowed me. As I closed it, the noise in the room exploded. Shouts of confusion could be heard while I and my friends sat there dazed. The ache in my skull did a double-time dance. When Adam finally stood, the rest of the room grew quiet.

"This meeting is to discuss the pending charges against *your* Forcers, Joan, not for you to file new charges," Adam said with a stern look at the woman across the aisle. "If the findings at the formal hearing don't clear up the actions of your Forcers, then another fact-finding investigation will take place."

"But Controller—" Joan started. She quickly stopped speaking when Adam held his hand up.

"You requested this meeting, and the committee agreed to it, but we will not open another investigation at this time when one has already been completed. If, after the hearing in three days' time, you are still not satisfied with the findings, a formal level-two investigation can take place. But know this—any further actions by your office to disrupt the lives of these students will be met with disciplinary action."

This threat must have meant something to Joan, as she quickly sat back down and folded her small hands on the table in front of her. I recalled studying the Forcers' chain of command in government class and remembered immediately that Joan's last name was Deller. She had been voted into the commander position over ten years ago. I tried to remember more, but whenever I thought, my head would start to pound again.

What followed were a lot of legal words, some of which I would look up later, some I never located because of my spelling or because I didn't remember them.

I was asked at one point if I knew who had attempted to conduct the search of my cubby, at which point the lawyer James stood and declared that my previous statements confirmed I had no memory of the request to search, only the memory of waking already on the floor, injured.

"Well, who do you claim put you there?" Primer Kasher asked, her brows furrowed together as she studied me. I stood and shrugged my shoulders. "I remember coming to and seeing Forcer Gunny there, but he was next to my bed. He only moved closer after I woke, but Tyler quickly came and stood over me. I know there were words spoken, but I was too out of it to remember what was said." I felt foolish for not even knowing what had actually happened. I should have asked my friends, or maybe this was a point for me, that I didn't know.

"Were you, at any point, informed of a search?" an older woman with short grey hair who was sitting at the end of the table asked.

"My friends said something about a search, but that was while I was in the hospital." Unfortunately, the word hospital caused some spit to come out of the missing gap in my teeth. I quickly wiped my chin and felt my face turn red from embarrassment.

"And did that happen from the incident?" the same woman asked as she pointed to my mouth.

"Yes," I said as another dribble of spit leaked out.

There was talk about my hospital visit and medical records, and the doctor's reports were reviewed, along with the "findings" of an investigation. After I finally sat back down, the questions were directed at a short man who was called forward from the back of the room.

I gathered he was the one who had conducted the investigation, but it wasn't until Evan whispered to me that I had a clearer picture of who the man was. "Todd Cooperson. He came to the dorm before you got released from the hospital."

Todd told the panel about who he had talked to, what he had discovered, and even items he had located. "I found two Z-riders located inside the Forcers' office the next day, after the attack." Todd presented a tag. "These have been turned over to the Primer office. As you can see, this one here"—he held up a photo and I caught a quick glance of my Z-rider—"is the original prototype and was confirmed to be Mr. Noman's."

"And who confirmed that?" Primer Kasher asked.

"Both Mr. Hudson and the other two boys. Also, I got confirmation from the Fixer hub, specifically the patent counsel, that Mr. Noman received a permit and certificate of authenticity several months ago." Todd once again handed several papers forward along the table.

"But isn't it true that Z-riders were no longer allowed on campus?" Primer Kasher asked with a frown. "So couldn't these have just been confiscated earlier in the day?"

"Actually, the rule states 'No private carts of any kind will be used,' the rule doesn't state anything about owning one. And I confirmed that there was no citation handed out by the Forcers for either Mr. Noman or Mr. Hudson for riding or *using* their Z-riders earlier in the day, so it was my conclusion that these two riders were taken at the time of the incident," Todd answered.

After the investigator was finished with his findings, each of my bunk mates was asked their story. But it wasn't until Tyler stood to relay his side of the tale that I got a clearer picture of what had really happened that night.

"Tyler Wilson," Tyler said as he stood tall before the table.

"Thank you," Primary Kasher said as she looked down at her tablet again. "Please tell us what you saw."

Since the Primary had been asking most of the questions, I suddenly wondered who the other people along the table were. I knew Adam Waltson, but other than that, I was left to speculate. However, I didn't have much time, as Tyler's account of events pulled me away from my thoughts soon after he started talking.

"The dorm advisors were all notified of the search of our building right after curfew," Tyler said, still standing tall with his hands at his side. "As instructed, I didn't notify any of the students assigned to my floor, and I made sure no one left."

"Yes, yes, what happened after the search started?" I wasn't sure, but I thought I heard a little impatience in Primary Kasher's voice.

"That's the thing," Tyler replied after clearing his throat. "The search didn't start until right after twenty-three hundred. I wasn't notified it would be so late and went to bed myself. After all, it was a school night." Tyler nodded to himself as if this justified why he'd gone to bed. "The Forcers were supposed to come to my room first, but I heard them banging along the stairs, and the big one—I mean, Forcer Woodson—demanded I show them to room three twenty-two. I thought this a strange request and wondered why they would start at the back of the building, but I immediately led them to the room." Here Tyler turned and gave me and my friends a sorrowful look. "There was no announcement. They didn't even turn the lights on until they were in the room. When I flashed the lights on, there was Z, I mean Zane, lying on the floor. There was a big hole in the wall above where he had just been thrown."

"Sorry, you said they announced themselves?" Primary Kasher asked as she moved to make a note on her tablet.

"No, ma'am. There was no formal or informal announcement. I heard Forcer Gunny call them little zits, then the crash of Zane hitting the wall," Tyler answered.

"And where were the other boys?" the woman at the end of the table asked.

"That's just it, ma'am." Tyler shook his head. "Z's bed is in the back of the room, past Evan's and Miles's cubbies. Both were still in bed, or just climbing out of their bunks, when I flashed on the lights."

"So you think Forcer Gunny passed them to get at Mr. Noman?" Adam Waltson asked as his tan eyes stared at the Forcers' Master Commander where she sat.

"Well, I do know there was some trouble involving Omar Gunnison and his friends last year in the Primer hub. Trouble that required Forcers and a hearing," Tyler said as he shook his head.

"You sure know a lot for a student," Primary Kasher said as she tapped one of her nails on the tablet.

"You think Forcer Gunny's action was retribution for the incident last year?" Adam Waltson asked, his eyes now turned to the Forcer in question.

"Could be," Tyler replied with a frown.

"I heard there was more trouble even after the lights were on," Adam stated, and he turned to study the dorm advisor, who turned beet red under his stare.

"Yes, sir. I was rushing forward to help Z when Forcer Gunny, fists raised, tried to round on my friend. It wasn't until I stood over Z and threatened Forcer Gunny with my grandfather's law firm that he finally backed off," Tyler said as his face turned even redder.

"That would be Wilson, Wilson, and Fitz?" the lady at the end of the table asked again.

"And James," our representative, James, added.

After Tyler was finished with his detailed story, there was more discussion, but by now my migraine had become almost unbearable. The lights, the noise, and probably the stress of the meeting caused me to feel ill.

Not wanting to throw up or faint in front of everyone, I quickly turned to Miles. "I'm not feeling well," I whispered, and to my mortification, Miles reached up and felt my forehead.

"Z, you're as white as a ghost," he said as the lights seeped into the back of my skull. I found each breath hard to suck in.

"Sir, I think Z needs to see a doctor," I heard Miles say.

"We won't be much longer," Primary Kasher said with a stern tone.

"We are done," Adam Waltson said suddenly. "This meeting is concluded, and the formal hearing will take place in three days' time. I think the boy needs to go back to the hospital hub."

The sound of chairs scraping along the floor was so loud that I thought my head would explode. I couldn't walk, so I sat there with my eyes closed, trying to block the light with my hands. That's when I heard the sound of heels clicking along the hard marble floor. The noise echoed in my mind, and I unwillingly returned to my nightmare once again.

"You know what this will do!" came the woman's high-pitched voice.

"I know what this means, to all of us," came the voice of Hudson Adamson.

"I only ask for more time," the woman had pleaded.

"How many thousands of years more do you need?" Hudson had demanded.

"Numbers must be run; we can't just throw this out there. Panic will ensue!"

"You don't get it. You don't grasp what this means." Frustration seeped out of Hudson's voice as I had tried to

hide further behind the ducting and pipes so I wouldn't be discovered where I wasn't allowed.

"I demand more time!" The female voice had sounded hysterical. "You will not tell him!"

"You don't own me. You may own others, but not me."

"I know your secrets!" the woman had threatened.

"And I know yours," Hudson had growled in response.

"You are no longer useful." This is what the woman had said seconds before she had killed Rafe's father, Hudson Adamson. She had killed him with a single shot to the chest with a blast gun.

Yet, as I sat there in the courtroom with my eyes closed and my hands still covering my face, it was the sound of the woman's heels walking past me that I feared more than the memory of the murder. Bracing for the pain, I moved my hands and opened my eyes in time to see Forcer Master Commander Joan Deller walking past me. The spikes of her high-heel shoes made the same sound they had made over a year ago down in the tunnels when she had run away after killing Rafe's father.

Chapter 11

Thoughts

I woke up in the hospital once again. It wasn't my first time here. The year before I had suffered from a burst appendix and had to remain for several days after my surgery.

Doctor Scottson was there, and he explained to me that I had passed out. He thought the strain of the trip and the meeting itself had been too much for my damaged head to take. But I knew it wasn't the concussion but the fact that I had finally discovered who had murdered Hudson Adamson.

Forcer Master Commander, the woman in charge of ECHO's police force, was a murderer. I didn't know why she had done it or what she and Hudson were doing in the tunnels that night. Nor did I understand what they had been talking about right before she had killed him.

After the doctor left me in my darkened room, I tried to think more about the murder, but the pain just grew stronger. After what seemed like hours, I checked the clock and realized it was the middle of the night. The hospital had grown quiet, and the faint glow from the nurses' station outside my room was the only source of light.

I suddenly envied my friends, who were probably back in our dorm room, sleeping comfortably, unaware of my dilemma. I didn't want to feel the pain in my head, nor did I want the knowledge of who had killed Rafe's father over a year ago. I didn't even want the memory of the murder. It still haunted me both in my sleep and in my waking hours.

As tears leaked out of my closed eyes, I felt a crushing shamefulness sweep over me. All of this had come from me slipping down into the tunnels, a place I had known I was forbidden to go.

It had been my recklessness that had brought me here. My sense of adventure had led me down a dark path where I'd witnessed the death of a man. And that had placed me in the path of his killer.

After my shame and self-pity wore off and the tears dried on my cheeks, I lay there in the hospital bed and thought. For some reason, I usually do my best thinking when I can't sleep in the dead of the night.

I pondered my life with Mia. My life in the Pipe hub had been hard. There had been accusations and demands for Mia to turn me over to another family so they could collect my credits. To pass me on and give me a life where I would have been allowed into the tunnels and trained in the Piper ways.

Why hadn't Mia done this? I could have been part of a larger family, raised to learn how to maintain the countless miles of tunnels containing pipes and ductwork that kept ECHO alive.

But if this had happened, I could have died like so many of the children of the Pipers. Kids who train with their parents down in the tunnels live a dangerous life. Some never make it out of the lower passageways. Others are injured or damaged from the dangers found in the underbelly of my home world.

After what seemed like hours, I came to the same conclusion I always did; I was glad Mia had kept me. Glad that she'd loved me enough to keep me to herself. Even with the knowledge that I would never be afforded a vocation, never be trained in the dangerous ways of the Pipes.

I knew it was Mia's decision that had brought me to where I was now and that gave me comfort. I reminded myself I wasn't alone. I had Mia, I had my new friends, and my best friend, Mitch.

Mitch! I had to tell him what I had discovered. He needed to know that I had found out who the murderer was.

I started to wonder about Joan Deller. I couldn't believe I had mistaken her for a young girl when I had seen her in the Printer hub almost a month before. It then dawned on me that maybe she had been there to check on me. But as I lay there, I couldn't comprehend why.

She probably knew about Mitch and his involvement. After all, I had accidentally left Mitch's hand-drawn map next to Hudson's body. Mitch had been questioned by Primary Kasher about the map. He had told her that he didn't know how his map had ended up in the tunnels. But we knew she didn't believe his lies, which is why we had to keep our friendship a secret.

Mitch had warned me that several professors kept asking him about friends. Thinking now, I wondered if the Primary had asked the professors to keep an eye on Mitch.

Suddenly my blood turned to ice as I thought of Joan Deller watching Mitch. Had she been in the Academy hub spying on us all along? Part of me doubted this, but I hadn't seen her approach me in the Printer hub. She had just suddenly been there, demanding my work order and permit.

I squeezed my eyes shut and thought back to that day. She hadn't even moved from the spot, but she also hadn't been wearing those ridiculously high heels. The sound echoed in my memory. Tap, tap and then a small click. I hadn't realized before the murder how important the sound of the woman fleeing was, until now. Until the tap, tap, click rang in my ears.

I needed to warn Mitch. Maybe Joan had already paid him a visit. If so, we both needed to continue to be on our guard.

As I lay there, surrounded by the darkened hospital, Hudson's words the night of his death came back to me. *"You don't own me. You may own others, but not me."* He had spoken these words to Joan before she had killed him. Had he meant the woman was blackmailing people? Maybe she had spies.

The realization came to me as sweat beaded on my forehead. Hudson had been speaking of spies and so had Mitch. My best friend had warned me about the professors keeping an eye on him. Hadn't he even cautioned me about Breanna when I had first become friends with her?

Afterall, Breanna was the Primary's daughter. But even sitting in the dark thinking scary thoughts, I couldn't imagine Breanna betraying me. Breanna was the head of EFAP, the group who were currently fighting for equality for the Pipers. If Breanna's mother found that out, I was sure the Primary would whisk Breanna out of school faster than I could spit.

No, Breanna wouldn't betray me. But she also didn't know my secrets. Only Mitch and Mia did.

With this thought I suddenly realized Mia needed to be warned too.

"Zap!" I hissed as I remembered Mia had a new Forcer friend. Forcer Brad Carrington had saved Mia and me last year. I had taken Mia into the main hub to pick up the new sewing machine I had bought her. We had just left the shop when Weston, Manny, and Omar had blocked our way. After a few punches, Forcer Brad had come to our rescue, or so I had thought. This was the very incident Tyler had mentioned in the meeting.

Maybe Brad was one of Joan's spies. Could he have been following us the whole time? I couldn't be sure and made a promise to myself to research Forcer Carrington when I was allowed to use electronic devices again.

The dangers seemed to surround me in the darkness of the hospital room. Every shadow appeared in my mind as an enemy, every whisper a secret. When I heard the shuffling of feet near my door, fear and panic left me paralyzed, and I quickly closed my eyes.

"Are you sure it was just stress?" Adam's voice drifted to me from beyond the hospital room.

"Yes. I have seen some of the photos and vids of the meeting. If the flashes were that strong, then I'm shocked he made it as long as he did," Doctor Scottson said. "Tell me, did she really try to file a claim against him?"

"Yes. We must be careful. There are rumors she has someone inside the hospital. Are you sure he's safe here?" Adam asked as I lay perfectly still, fearful a twitch or movement might give it away that I was awake and listening.

"I or my wife will remain on duty until he is returned to campus. But what about his safety there?" Dr. Scottson asked, and I heard concern in his voice.

"I think his friends have already proven they can watch

out for him. And Rafe is there," Adam said. "No one will dare attack one that holds my name."

I heard them move away from my door and let out a quick breath, one I hadn't known I had been holding.

Zap, Adam knew. Adam knew Joan Deller was dangerous. I looked towards the open doorway.

My private benefactor had not only set up my school funding, but it appeared he had set up security to keep me safe from the very woman who had killed his son.

By the time I returned to my dorm room, I had a list of questions and zero answers. I had also formulated a plan, but it would take me some time to put it into action.

First, I had to warn Mitch.

Second, I had to warn Mia, but I had to do this without her Forcer friend knowing or finding out.

Third, I had to somehow let Adam know who had killed his son. And I had to do this without him discovering who was providing the information, or that I was the one who had witnessed the death of Hudson.

Each time I came up with a plan of action, I thought of more problems, more limitations. Danger, it appeared, came with each step of my plan. The first, I hoped, would be easy. Mitch would be sitting beside me in each of our classes. But if there were spies, and if the spies were professors, then I couldn't just tell Mitch my discovery while in class.

The first night back in the dorm, I wished for my missing TWT. I knew Mitch's warning had saved us. I didn't know how he knew, but I was glad he'd told me in time for me to dismantle my talking device. I didn't know where the pieces had ended up. Probably with my missing Z-rider in the Primary's office.

By the time I fell asleep that night, I had formulated a strategy to tell Mitch. It would be a two-step plan, one that required me to tell him I had a secret while in class and tell him what it was when we were alone, maybe during our tutoring sessions.

I arrived in class that day and felt confident in my plan. In base class, however, my idea failed. I discovered that Professor Luthier had changed my seat to the front of the class.

"I hope you are feeling better. I have strict instructions to keep a close eye on you," Professor Luthier told me as she looked down her narrow nose at me as if I might faint any minute.

The second class wasn't much easier. Professor Bradson didn't let me sit in front of a computer, but instead had me sit at his desk while Mitch sat at his normal terminal and kept notes for me.

Mitch didn't have programing, so Miles took my notes, as I was once again restricted to a non-screen desk while in the class.

By lunch, my frustration was almost as high as the pain in my head. I worried I wouldn't get to warn Mitch, nor ever speak privately with him again.

"Here, Mom said you might need a pain pill by now," Mitch told me as he set a white pill on my plate.

I studied the pill for a second then quickly swallowed it with my drink. I didn't want to imagine the rest of the day with the pain I was feeling now.

I saw Mitch walking over and leaning forward a little. Instead of waiting for him to come to me, I downed my drink and stood, glass in hand, on the pretense that I was going to refill it.

"I'll be right back," I told my friends, and I intercepted Mitch halfway across the room.

"Walk with me," I told him and held up my now empty glass.

"I wanted to remind you about—" Mitch started, but I quickly quieted him.

"Shh, listen." I made a show of pointing at my glass and the line for the drinks. "I have something important to tell you. No, not here," I hissed as my eyes swiveled around the room. I had noticed several professors sitting near the food line and couldn't take a chance to tell Mitch my secret here, no matter what. "Listen, our tutoring session is tonight. I need you to make an excuse and send everyone home early. I have to talk to you alone," I insisted. "It's about what I saw you know when."

Mitch nodded his head once and said loudly, "Very well, I will have your notes during our session tonight. But I may need to keep you longer than the others as there will be more subjects to cover." With this, Mitch turned and hobbled away using his crutches. Once again, I made a note to raise his crutches the next time I saw him so he wouldn't have to lean so far forward. Then I moved a step up in the line to refill my drink

The pain pill worked on my head, and my remaining three classes flew by. Thank goodness mechanics class didn't use any screens. However, accounting was difficult without the screen, and since the numbers made my eyes hurt, I was told to let Mitch show me later that night. The last class of the day was my government class. It was all lecture and no screens, so I didn't miss much.

The school day drew to an end, and I had a whole hour before dinner, so I moved on to the next phase of my plan. Warning Mia.

I had thought of using a message pod, but those could be intercepted. Even E-notes weren't private. I thought of sending a coded message, but worried Mia wouldn't understand any code I could think of. Instead, I checked the calendar and realized we were less than one month away from Launch Day. Students would be allowed to return home for the holiday, and I felt it would be safe to wait and tell Mia then.

That left telling Adam. Rafe knew how to get ahold of his grandfather, but I didn't. If only I had seen Adam again while I had been in the hospital. But the more I thought of that, the more I realized I was glad I hadn't spoken up that night. If I had told Adam, then he would have known it was me who had been with his son that night in the tunnels.

It would be better if I sent a private, secret message to him. Maybe I could leave a message for him in a place only he could go. If I could get into the secret monitor room again... But I couldn't. I tried numerous times during school break. Nor could I get into the Fixer hub for several months.

Unless...

I wondered if Evan and I could go to his parents' house that coming weekend. Maybe I could somehow talk my friends into visiting the workshop? Plans formed in my brain as I waited for dinner time and tried to complete some of my homework. When dinner time did come, we all walked to the kitchen hall together, and I voiced my idea.

"Miles, how are our sales numbers?" I asked as we left our dorm building.

"Good. Now that Z-riders are allowed back on campus, all of our lost sales have returned. Our wait list is now twice as long as it was prior to the start of school. It actually appears that the incident caused our sales to soar," he replied with a smile.

"Then maybe we should spend this weekend building?" I smiled when Evan agreed with me.

"Don't forget we have the trial tomorrow, but maybe afterwards, instead of returning to campus, we can just head over to the workshop," Rafe suggested.

When we entered the kitchen hall, the entire hall grew quiet. We all stopped and looked around, confused by the sudden silence. We turned when Breanna rushed up to us. Her face was white and her eyes huge with shock.

"Z, I just heard the news," she said, a little breathless. She grabbed my arm. "Z, they found Forcer Woodson dead."

All eyes turned to me.

Chapter 12

Darkness

Forcer Woodson's body had been found in his home early that morning. The rumor going around school was that he had hung himself. There was speculation that he feared the outcome of the pending trial. Rumors hinted that the verdict would not favor him nor his co-worker Forcer Gunny Brackson, who now couldn't be located.

A message from Head Dean was waiting for us in our dorm room when we got back from dinner.

"Sorry, boys, it appears the trial has been delayed until further notice," was all the E-pod had said.

When I left the dorm for Mitch's, my friends were still talking about the situation. Miles and Evan kept throwing questions and speculation at Rafe and Tyler about what would happen now to our trial.

"Do you think Forcer Gunny will be found?" Evan asked Rafe, who shrugged his shoulders as I stepped out into the hall. As I made my way to Mitch's that night, I thought about the news.

If Forcer Woodson had killed himself, could it have

been from guilt? Something in me said no. I remembered the sour face he had made during the meeting; it hadn't spoken of guilt or even remorse.

I had just passed the third building when another thought came to me. What if the Forcer hadn't killed himself? What if Master Commander Joan Deller had killed him? After all, she had killed before. This thought had the hair on my neck standing on end, and I quickly glanced around as I hastened my steps.

Every dark shadow seemed to move; every corner held danger. When sounds floated down the almost empty streets, I thought I could hear the sound from a blast gun.

By the time I reached Mitch's building, I was outright running. My heart was pounding in my head, and I had a layer of sweat on my face. Taking time to wipe my forehead, I took two deep breaths before I entered the building and knocked on his door.

The usual students from last year were inside, except there was a new girl who was at level one. After the first hour, three kids left and within another fifteen minutes, Mitch and I were finally left alone.

"I know we don't have much time, but Mitch, I know who the killer is," I said immediately after the last student, a kid named Brian, had left, and I had securely shut the door behind him.

"What?" Mitch asked as he reached out and squeezed my arm.

It took me ten minutes to tell him my discovery. He doubted me at first, but I told him of my conversation with Joan in the Printer hub. Then the conversation I had overheard in the hospital between Adam and the doctor, which is when he finally nodded.

"So, Adam might know about the danger?" Mitch asked. I shrugged in reply.

"He said I would be safe there, that Miles's mom and dad were watching over me," I said with a frown. "He also said I should be safe at school because Rafe was there."

"Zap. This is big! Forcer Master Commander is a high-level position." Mitch shook his head. "Zane, this is huge."

"What should we do? I want to warn Mia. I *need* to warn her," I amended. "I also need to let Adam know."

"What?" Mitch exclaimed. "No! No, you can't." He shook his head and reached over and grabbed my arm again. "No, the danger is too great!"

"I think she already tried to kill me," I said suddenly and told Mitch about the scare I had in the Fixer hub during school break.

"Are you sure?" he asked, looking at me with speculation. "Did you see a gun?"

"No, I didn't see anything," I said with a frown. "I only heard a loud pop. But I was so scared. I hadn't been that terrified since I discovered Hudson down in the tunnels."

Mitch didn't want me to take any action in either warning Mia or trying to talk to Adam. At least not until he had time to think.

"I know several of the professors are watching me. At least Professor Ricker and Larson are keeping close. Ricker keeps asking me questions, and Larson won't let me eat alone."

I hadn't heard of Professor Larson before but knew now that Mitch was correct, there had to be spies in the Academy. I knew for sure that there were spies in the hospital. Adam had said as much.

I left Mitch's that evening with his notes and thought of my plan for how I would warn my grandmother, yet I still didn't know how I would inform Adam of my discovery. I left at a dead run and didn't stop until I made it safely to my dorm building.

The second month of school came and went. The trial had been delayed indefinitely and there was still no news about locating Manny's father nor anything more about the suicide of Forcer Woodson.

When my concussion limitations had been lifted and my tooth replaced, I settled back into the daily routine of school, with the exception of riding my Z-rider. Miles's mother didn't think I was ready for that.

My rider and Rafe's had been returned to us a week before. Mine had a flat tire, and Rafe's needed a new memory board. But we spent a weekend in the Fixer hub doing repairs and building new riders to fill the orders, which were now returning to a high volume. Credits were rolling in now that the Academy rules had been lifted.

My big plan to send an anonymous note to Adam via the Fixer hub had been set aside. Mitch and I had talked each study session, and we both agreed the dangers were too high to try something foolish without thinking it through first.

We had dismissed sending a message pod, an email, and even a paper note, something I had thought about doing while in the Fixer hub. I thought I could type a message and maybe slip it under the hidden door to the monitor room. But Mitch quickly pointed out that Adam knew I knew about that room.

"Hadn't you been following him when you discovered that room?" Mitch had asked.

"Well, I didn't actually see him enter the corridor," I had whined, but in the end, Mitch's warnings made sense.

Mia still needed to be warned, but the celebration of Launch Day was in two days, something I was looking forward to. I hadn't spent much time in my home hub for several months, and I was getting homesick. I missed Mia, her home-cooked meals and her company.

She had sent me care packages, and we exchanged E-letters on a regular basis, but I yearned to hear her opinion of my discoveries.

I had finished getting dressed and had joined the others near our dorm door so we could head over for breakfast when Tyler met us in the hallway.

"Z, you have a note from the dean." He handed me the message pod with a frown on his face. "I fear it's not good news."

"What do you mean?" I asked, frowning down at the glowing yellow orb, which indicated it contained a message.

"I heard there was an attack last night in the main hub. Sounds like it got nasty," Tyler said as Rafe cleared his throat.

"Attack?" Fear and worry filled me until Evan spoke up.

"He means in the Primer hub." Evan gave Tyler a shove. "Thanks for delivering the message."

"Attack, what attack?" I asked, but Tyler was already rounding the corner to the elevator. I turned and saw all three of my bunkmates avoiding my eyes. "What attack?" I demanded, the pod still in my fisted hand.

Rafe cleared his throat then slumped his shoulders. "He'll find out soon enough," he said, and when his eyes met mine, my fear increased. "EFAP had a peaceful demonstration last night," he started, but he was interrupted by Miles.

"It didn't end up peaceful." When my eyes turned to Miles, his frown increased, and he quickly looked down at his shoes.

"What?" I asked again.

"Well," Rafe said with a loud sigh, "several people stood up to the Forcers who were called in. Much like what you saw when we went to the court meeting, but..."

"Someone brought a pipe, just to show their support. But things got out of hand," Evan finished.

"Three people ended up in the hospital," Miles supplied. "One Forcer and two administrative employees."

Turning my eyes away from my friends, I looked down at the message pod. I clicked it, and we all heard as the Head Dean's voice floated out.

"It is with regret that I must inform you that your travel plans to the Pipe hub have been temporarily denied. All travel in and out of the Pipes is being blocked to the Primary's office. Please let my office know if you wish to visit another hub for this coming holiday. Thank you, Head Dean Dick Dickson."

Evan invited me to stay with his family for the weeklong holiday. At first, I thought about staying at school, but that thought was too depressing, so I agreed to join him in the Fixer hub.

I had ideas about spending most of my time building riders and sleeping in the workshop. However, when Evan and I arrived at his parents' place, those ideas left my mind.

Evan's mother, Marline, had their home decorated with Launch Day–themed decorations. There were little rocket ships, orbs, and bright stars hanging from the ceiling. A model of ECHO sat on the dining room table, which was also piled with food.

Evan's father, Alder, had moved most of his unfinished projects over to the workshop, which Marline kept mentioning with a big smile.

"The house hasn't been this uncluttered since we moved in," she said with a smile in her dark brown eyes. She gave me a wink. "I can't thank you enough for letting Alder take up your lease while you are at school."

"Dad kept our stuff; we have one table and two employees still making Z-riders," Evan said quickly. "But that doesn't leave us much room."

The week I spent at Evan's home was amazing. We had dinner the first night at their home, but after that the party spread out into the streets of the Fixer hub. The streets were littered with tables piled with food. Neighbors and friends invited anyone and everyone into their homes.

Men sat around talking inventions while children ran around with laser lights, playing games. Bright orange and blue lights flashed everywhere as sounds of laughter and joy rang out on every street.

In the Pipe hub, our celebrations were mild compared to what I witnessed in the Fixer hub that week. The abundance of food and the relaxed atmosphere were foreign to me. Yet, I enjoyed every minute of it.

Returning to school seemed a chore, but it was one I quickly settled back into. I had three letters from Mia waiting for me when I returned. Each letter spoke of the unrest inside the Pipe hub.

Most, it seemed, didn't understand why they were being restricted to their hub. Not that many Pipers traveled outside the home hub but supplies and medical appointments had been postponed or cancelled due to the restrictions.

Mia spoke of Forcer Brad twice and mentioned that he hadn't been allowed inside the Piper hub either. This fact gave me hope, and I felt a wave of relief sweep into me until I read her next sentence. *"I'm so lonely without you or Brad."*

Guilt swept over me, and it mixed with worry for my grandmother. If Master Commander Joan had attempted to shoot at me when I had been in the Fixer hub all those months ago, then what would stop her from going after my grandmother?

Sitting down, I opened my school tablet and had a message half written to Mia before I stopped. I couldn't just write to her and warn her. I had to think, but I hadn't come up with any ideas for several months now and I suddenly became frustrated.

All communications could be traced or intercepted by Joan. I had to get a message to Mia that couldn't be understood, something that warned her of danger.

I deleted my original message and carefully typed a new, very short one.

Mia,

I spent my holiday with Evan's family in the Fixer hub. They have so many inventions there. Some remind me of my first one. Remember the last time I used it? I have recently found its missing piece and wanted you to know.

Carefully yours,

Zane.

Confident that my message was cryptic enough, I hit send and got my stuff ready for class, which would start again the next morning.

Before breakfast, I received a reply.

Zane,

I'm glad you had fun with Evan's family. I am well and excited you located the item. Remember to wear your safety cap when riding.

Cautiously and with love,

Mia.

I understood her warning. She wanted me to be careful. Quickly I sent another message letting her know I loved her and went off to class feeling relief that at least Mia was now warned of danger.

Upon returning to school after the break, I had received my grades. I had passing numbers, though I thought my grade in my new environmentalist class was a little low. I was pleased to see my focus and concentration in government class had awarded me a higher grade. That class, along with architect class, were now my highest grades.

The Pipe hub was opened two weeks later. It would have remained closed, but there had been an accident involving a faulty recycling air duct in the hospital portion of the hub.

Three people had lost consciousness and two had electrical burns after an air duct had locked in the closed position. A repair man from the Fixer hub had tried to crawl down inside but had managed to break the duct even more.

This incident was only one of several caused by the restriction the Pipers were facing. Nothing would have changed except the head of the hospital, an elder man named Berenson, had sent a formal complaint to the Primary. His grievance spoke of the dangers ECHO would face if the Pipers weren't able to return to their normal functions.

When the tunnel into the Pipe hub was opened again, it came with a new requirement. Passes had to be acquired and were only granted after a full review of the request was completed by the Primary's office.

Mia had been denied a pass out of the Piper hub, but I had gotten one for Colony Day, which would take place in just over a month.

After receiving this pass, I was telling Evan and Miles the good news when Breanna approached us in the kitchen hall. I hadn't been able to spend much time with her because of the new seating assignments, but we had been passing notes back and forth during mealtimes. She had explained to me that she wasn't allowed to sit with me anymore, as her mother had found out about our prior contact, probably from the dean.

As Breanna approached, she gave me a weak smile and handed me a crumpled paper, then quickly walked away again. Knowing even the passing of a note might get back to her mother, I quickly tucked the paper into my pocket and finished eating.

It wasn't until I returned to my dorm and the privacy of my cubby that I pulled the paper from my pocket. I had to read it three times before it's meaning sunk in.

Your warning was received. Know that she is protected now.

Brad.

Chapter 13

Ruling

My worry for Mia increased the more I thought about Brad's note. I tried to call her immediately after receiving it, but she didn't pick up. I sent her another message but didn't receive an answer by the next morning. The lack of communication from her doubled my worry.

I knew she wasn't allowed outside the Pipe hub, and neither were any other Pipers. What little news I could pull up from ECHO's two channels spoke only about Launch Day celebrations in the main hub. There wasn't any coverage about Pipers and the hub's new restrictions.

When school was over that day, I rushed back to my cubby and to my huge relief saw a message waiting in my personal email. I held my breath as I opened it but was filled immediately with disappointment when I saw it was a formal notice from the Primer hub.

As I was opening it, I heard Rafe and Miles talking. It wasn't until Evan came over and stood next to me that I realized they were trying to get my attention.

"Z," Evan said as he stood behind me. "Hey, he got one

too." The attachment had just opened when Rafe came over and joined us.

"What does yours say?" Rafe asked as I leaned closer to the screen. It was an official document and as Rafe read it over my shoulder, I squinted my eyes at it.

"What is adjudication?" I asked.

"I'll go get Tyler," Miles said as he quickly raced from the room.

I stopped reading beyond the first sentence. The words did not make any sense to me, and the only sentence I could understand was the one where our names were all listed in a tidy row.

"Here he is," Miles exclaimed as Tyler came in and stood behind me.

"Oh, they made a decision," Tyler said. He quickly read through the document. Occasionally he would mutter to himself or make an odd noise in his throat. When I couldn't stand the tension any longer, I finally asked him what it all meant.

"Well, it says a lot of things. The main point is that the hearing was held." Tyler continued to study my screen.

"What? Without us?" Rafe demanded.

"Yes, well, it appears the panel used our informal meeting notes to make their decision. Since neither Forcer could be present, and with the untimely death—their words not mine—of Forcer Simon Woodson, they decided to just complete their ruling. It was found that the office of the Forcer Master Commander was at fault in the incident. Z, your medical bills have been paid. Two hundred units have been awarded to you and half that amount to the other three listed in this suit. The Academy was also awarded damages, and the Forcers located here have been retracted."

"What does that mean, retracted?" I asked in confusion.

"Well, each hub has their own Forcers. Men or women who have been trained for the job but are also from that hub. This hub has ten people who hold this position. However, the Forcer Master Commander's office has twenty additional Forcers who are assigned to each hub. These Forcers are from the main hub." Tyler stood straight and looked at me. "I thought you knew this?"

"My hub has only two. On the weekends I think we have a few more, but I never knew where they came from," I admitted as I tried to read some of the document again.

"Why were we given so little?" Rafe's question interrupted my thoughts.

"Little?" I squeaked.

"Most class action suits result in a higher penalty. However, since the action was on the Academy grounds, the findings were limited by the school's policy," Tyler explained.

"Two hundred credits aren't a little amount," I mumbled.

"It's not credits," Tyler said as he turned to look at me. "It's units. Each unit is a hundred credits."

My head swam as I thought about the amount of funds I was being awarded. Even with my income from the Z-riders, I had yet to reach one hundred credits. Mia and I could live comfortably off the funds I had acquired from the riders, but now we had two hundred units. This thought almost caused me to hyperventilate.

"Does it say anything about Forcer Gunny?" Evan asked. "Has he shown up?"

After Tyler read the entire document, he confirmed that there was no news about Forcer Gunny.

The legal document had been sent to Mia and the other

boys' parents. Before dinner that night, I finally heard from her.

"Zane, did you receive a copy of the notice?" she wrote.

"I did. Tyler says we won over two hundred units. Mia, each unit is worth a hundred credits," I typed back quickly. "How safe are you?" I asked my need to ensure her safety outweighing my privacy concerns.

"I just checked, and the credits are there. I can't believe it. I have never seen so much in my life. I am safe. Brad is here with me now. He got special permission to join the Pipe Forcers and is living two streets down, for now."

This news didn't sit well with me. I was trying to warn her about the Forcers, specifically their boss.

"Mia." I didn't know how to proceed. If I told her I didn't trust Brad, then she would demand to know why. I finally settled on replying with the truth. "Remember, it was Forcers who hurt me."

"Brad saved us once before," she wrote. "He knows your struggles."

She was silent after this, and I read her message twice before the guys finally nagged me to leave for dinner.

I couldn't wait for the holiday. I had so much to tell Mia, to warn her about. Every day I spent away from her had new fears growing in my mind. I had visions of Mia being shot, lying in a pool of her own blood, much as Hudson Adamson had done that night so long ago in the tunnels beneath ECHO.

My nightmares increased the week before I was to journey home. I would wake in a cold sweat and feel sick when I remembered the details of my dreams.

When the day finally came to journey home, I was already waiting outside the dorm building when Financial Advisor Mathew Carlson drove up in a cart.

"Ah, I see you are most anxious to travel home," he said with a smile.

I threw my little bag into the back seat and sat next to Mathew with a sigh. "I haven't been home for months now."

"I know. Such sad affairs keeping the Piper hub closed." He started the cart. "There's just no need for such drastic measures."

As we exited the Academy hub and traveled through the Primer hub, Mathew talked of the injustices the Pipers were being dealt. He spoke of the shame the Primer should be feeling about shutting down the lifeblood of ECHO. I listened with half an ear as I thought of what I would tell Mia. How I should warn her and let her know who the murderer was.

By the time we reached the tunnel into the Pipes, I had myself all worked up. It wasn't until the cart stopped that I realized there was a new blockade preventing us from entering my home hub's entrance tunnel.

"Ah, I'm afraid this is as far as I'm allowed," Mathew said as he turned to look at me. "Do you have your papers? Good," he said as I held up the pass. "I will come and get you in three days' time. I'm afraid that's all your pass is good for this trip. Maybe next time it can be extended." He shook his head. "Just show the Forcers your pass. I expect they will do a search of your bag, but you should be fine after that."

The smile he gave me was meant to be reassuring, but I felt my palms go damp when four large Forcers approached us. One of them was Forcer Brad Carrington, who had a wide smile on his face as he walked towards me. The blood in my veins turned ice cold as I sat there helplessly and watched the large man draw near.

•   •   •

"I've got this one," Forcer Brad said as he walked towards me. The three other Forcers returned to their temporary station before I had even built up the courage to climb out of the cart. Brad grabbed my bag from the back seat as Mathew elbowed me in the ribs.

"Better get a move on," Mathew said with a smile. "Show them your papers. You'll be fine."

I hadn't had any occasion to be near Forcers since my attack and finding myself facing four now had my heart racing. Even knowing one of them personally didn't help.

"Um," was all I managed as I exited the cart.

"Just a quick glance in your bag is all I need," Brad said with another smile. "I actually am on break now and was hoping to walk you home. Mia and I have..." He suddenly stopped talking and shrugged his large shoulders once. "She is excited to see you," he said finally. His cheeks went slightly pink, which confused me.

My bag was inspected while Mathew turned the cart around and headed back down the tunnel. Then Brad handed me my sack and turned to guide me through the barrier. Its flashing orbs lit up the entrance to my home.

Immediately recognizable smells wafted to me, so familiar they almost caused me to cry. The smell of grease and mixed spices reminded me of my childhood. I saw familiar homes and walkways, and even a burned-out light high along one wall was endearing to me.

We walked the three long blocks to my home in silence. Occasionally I saw a familiar face. Old man Grayson waved to me as we walked past him. But no one stopped to speak with me, probably because I was in the presence of a Forcer from the main hub.

I didn't know what to say as the silence continued to

hang between us. Brad was two feet taller than me, and with his wide shoulders I felt small and vulnerable.

When we got to the front door of my home, he moved to knock, but I reached for the knob and swung it open, shouting for my grandmother.

"Mia, I'm home," I said as I flung my bag towards where the couch used to be. When it hit the ground, I turned to look at my bag on the floor while my grandmother came rushing in from the back room. The moved furniture wasn't the only change. Mia had her short hair curled, and her lips were bright pink. She wore a pretty dress, and her eyes were painted, much like the girls at school did.

"Zane!" Mia said as she embraced me. I felt a sigh of relief wash over me as I hugged her back. She was safe, and I was home. She smelled wonderful, and tears stung my eyes as I squeezed her tightly.

"Brad, thank you for bringing him," Mia said, wrapping her arms around the Forcer.

My shock spread when Brad placed a gentle kiss on Mia's lips. My grandmother's cheeks turned a bright pink as her eyes darted over to me.

"Um, Zane, there's something we have to tell you," Mia started, and suddenly I desperately wished I had remained at school. "Brad and I are engaged." With these words, a buzzing filled my ears and my heart dropped down to rest somewhere near the bottom of my stomach.

If Mia had told me she was recently elected to replace the Primary, I wouldn't have been as shocked as I was now, hearing that my grandmother would soon be married to the large Forcer.

Mia was old, I thought. She was my grandmother, and she wasn't supposed to be in a romantic relationship. My brain couldn't wrap around this thought as I sat in the front room and listened to the two tell me how they had been corresponding since Brad had rescued us from Weston and his two goons.

"I asked my commander if I could lead the new Forcer patrol inside the Pipe hub. I had to pull some strings, but with my history, well..." Brad said as he sat next to Mia on the couch, which now rested against the far wall. The whole room had been shuffled, and Mia's sewing supplies filled the small cubby in the far corner near the hall leading to the back rooms. The usually familiar room felt foreign to me as I sat there and listened to them.

"Zane, Brad has helped me with so much during these last months. I've been lonely since the hub was shut down. "And, well, he's been here for me," Mia explained as Brad placed his massive arm around her shoulders. "He's kept an eye on me, ensuring I'm safe."

What could I say? I wanted to shout at her that it was his boss who had killed Hudson over a year ago. That if Brad worked for Joan Deller, he couldn't be trustworthy. But I couldn't. Not with Brad sitting on the couch making googly eyes at my grandmother.

I mumbled congratulations and remained silent about my worries, for now. This must have appeased her, as she smiled and then asked about school and my health.

After I told her I was fine, she stood to help me unpack. Brad remained for a few more minutes but then left, as he was expected back at the barrier. Mia had made plans to celebrate that evening with a special dinner, and Brad had told her he would be back later to help prepare the food. This shocked me a little, but I waited until he had gone ten minutes before I rounded on Mia.

"Mia, we need to talk." I turned the radio on and sat next to it. I motioned her over and leaned forward and told her everything. I explained how I had discovered Forcer Master Commander Joan Deller was the killer of Hudson Adamson.

"Are you sure?" she demanded as she grabbed my hands.

"Mia, I heard her. It wasn't until she was walking on the marble flooring that I knew for sure. But when I saw her before in the Printer hub, I didn't hear her walk, she just stood there." I shook my head. "I admit, it wasn't her voice that reminded me, but I know. Mia, she's the one who killed him."

Mia remained silent for several seconds, deep in thought. I too remained quiet, knowing by how she held herself that she was weighing options and ideas.

"Mia, we have to warn Adam Waltson," I finally urged. "He has to know!"

She nodded her head, but there was worry in her eyes. "How?" She squeezed my hands. "How do we do that without giving ourselves away?"

Part of my worry melted away. I was no longer alone. Mia was there, like she always was. And I knew she would help me figure out the next step.

"Brad!" Mia suddenly said with a smile. "He can help."

"No!" I barked and then told Mia my worries about the Forcer.

"No, he's not like that," Mia insisted. "He wouldn't betray me. He has done nothing but protect me since that day in the Primer hub."

She was convinced that we should tell Brad about our concerns. Nothing I said would change her mind, and she urged me to trust her judgment in the matter.

"We will tell him, later tonight, after dinner," she urged. "He will know how we can warn Adam."

Chapter 14

Celebration

Three of our relatives stopped by during the day. Two were cousins, and they stayed for a while to ask me about school. The third was only there for an order pickup from Mia.

"Mia, why are you still working?" I asked after the last relative had left. "The money we got from my attack is more than enough to allow us to live comfortably. You don't need to work anymore."

"Oh, it's not about money," Mia said as she picked up the drinking glasses our guests had used. "I know we don't need the money; in fact, I lowered my rates quite a bit." She looked at me with a half-smile on her lips. "Don't you see? The kids still need clothing, and there's no other way for them to obtain it."

"You mean because the hub has been closed?" I raised my hands in a helpless gesture.

"That's only part of it." She turned her back on me while she wiped off the little table in front of the couch.

"Well, what then?" I asked.

"It's true, the hub being closed has limited the supply

chain. But the costs are also very high for new garments. And, well, people just can't afford to buy new clothes for their children. I want to continue because it's needed."

I felt my pride for Mia grow, but then it mixed with frustration. What was the revolution doing? How did it really help? I stood there in my home and saw all of the limitations. Control of our lives had been taken from us. Travel beyond our hub was limited, and we could barely feed and clothe ourselves.

I saw understanding in Mia's eyes as she turned back to look at me. With a nod, she embraced me. Loved swelled inside my chest and, despite all the limitations, I felt very rich. It was then that I realized that love often replaced what one was lacking in possessions.

True to his word, Brad came back just as Mia was starting the special dinner. I was surprised and pleased to see the large man actually help with the cooking.

The small pot of my favorite stew was steaming over the hot plate, and Brad was sitting at the table rolling out the flat cakes while I chopped the cubes of sugar for the dessert.

We ate the excellent meal as Brad told us about his time in the main hub. I hadn't known that he had served as a private guard for the Primary several years before.

"So, you know Breanna?" I asked.

"I first met her when she was little. We still keep in touch." Brad cast a look over at Mia, who nodded. I studied the two as I set my spoon down.

"What?" I demanded.

"Zane," Mia started, but she stopped when Brad placed his hand over hers.

"I will do it," Brad said softly, turning to study me. "Breanna and I are in regular communication. You see, I was the one she asked to lead the movement."

I could actually hear the pounding of my heart in my ears as Brad finished talking. "You?" I heard horror and shock in my voice but, instead of being offended, Brad let out a loud laugh.

"Yes. I too was shocked. But she had learned about my involvement in the incident you two had last year. She knew me and since I had been her guard only three years before, she knew how to get ahold of me. After she contacted me, I thought about it for only a day, then I agreed."

"He has been most helpful." Mia placed her other hand over Brad's on the table. "Even here he has made a difference."

"Difference?" I asked, shaking my head. The last I heard; the hub had been locked down. How could one man help?

"I was able to talk the Primary's office into continuing supply deliveries during the lockdown," Brad said as he looked at me. "The office in charge was the hub command post. They had been told to stop all deliveries. But that would have put all of ECHO in danger." He shook his head. "The idiots didn't even realize how important the Pipe hub is."

"Most don't," I said with understanding.

"It's shocking," Mia said with a shake of her head.

"Two days after the lockdown, I was able to start the supply run again. There was a small accident down in the tunnels, but Mia said no one was badly hurt. I used that as an example of why it's important to maintain supply runs. It was at that point that I was asked to lead the units who were moved into the Pipes. Mia and I were already communicating then, and I quickly agreed."

"And the movement?" I asked.

"Well, nothing has happened here in the Pipes, of course, but several meetings have taken place in the main hub. We now have a banker, two low-level politicians, and six high-level clerks who are taking up the fight. Two of them are now in charge of the leaflets."

"Leaflets?" I asked with fear and a little awe.

"They help us recruit more members," Brad said with a smile.

"Zane, this is what I meant when I said you can trust Brad," Mia said with a stern look towards me. "I think you should tell him our struggles," she urged.

I studied the man sitting across from me. He had a large Forcer build, but the look in his soft brown eyes spoke of understanding and kindness. His large hand rested comfortably inside Mia's small ones and when he gave me an encouraging smile, I conceded and sighed.

There in the low light of my grandmother's dining area, I told Brad about my nightmare. I spoke of how I had slipped down into the tunnels for several years and how I had witnessed the murder of a man, a man I later identified as Hudson Adamson.

I relayed my recent discovery and belief that it was Forcer Master Commander Joan Deller who had actually killed Hudson down in the tunnels under ECHO.

To his credit, Brad sat silently during my whole story. It wasn't until I reached this part that he leaned forward with his eyes wide and shock all over his face.

"Are you sure?" he demanded.

"I've had nightmares since the murder, and one thing is constant in each dream," I explained. "I can always hear the killer walking away. It's this unique sound that confirmed to me that she is the killer."

"And you heard it, I mean you heard her steps, in the

meeting room during the briefing?" Brad asked. I nodded my head.

I was expecting an argument from him, but I saw acceptance in his eyes as he leaned back and scratched his chin.

"Then we need to find a way to warn Adam. If she's willing to kill his son, there's no doubt that she would go after him too."

Colony Day came and with it the usual celebrations. There were parties to attend, thrown by distant cousins of Mia's and two old friends whom she had known from childhood. One had survived a tunnel collapse before I was born and was still unable to leave her home. She was no longer bedridden but sat on a large chair in the front room of her small home. Her damaged legs were tucked under a thick patched quilt, an evil reminder of the dangers of my home hub's vocation.

Mia also had friends and family stop by after our outings, and Mia presented each with a bag as they departed. This was something new, as we usually couldn't afford to give gifts. When she wasn't looking, I peeked in and saw several items of clothing along with a gift of baked bread and other foods. After this, I helped her hand out the bags.

I was excited to see Mitch and his family show up, though I still hadn't forgiven Mitch's mom for telling Advisor Jeffson that I might know something about what had happened down in the tunnels after Hudson's body was discovered. If Waltson hadn't called during the middle of the interrogation, Mia and I both could have been in real trouble.

I was able to spend some time with Mitch alone, and I

showed him my newest invention, a toy that flashed lights in a pattern. At each level, the pattern got harder.

"It's helped me a little with coding class. I keep forgetting the meaning of colors used for wires," I told him with a shrug. "I hope to incorporate the code sounds, but I still haven't worked that out yet."

Mitch gave me some ideas for how to mix a sound cube with my light toy, and I was still working on it when his family left.

During dinner that night Brad told me his idea for sending Adam Waltson a message.

"When I go for my weekly report meeting in the main hub, I can drop a message cube to my contact there. They can then send an anonymous message to the Controller's office," Brad explained.

"He has an office?" I asked.

"Well, I've never heard of him, but if he was at your hearing, then he must have an office somewhere," Brad explained.

We spent the rest of that evening searching online for the Controller's office. Brad had special privileges that allowed him access to the Prime hub's grid map. There were details of current office locations and even a list of employees who worked in each building.

What was missing, to our frustration, was any sign of Adam Waltson.

I had to return to the Academy the following day. My farewell to Mia was a sad one. She hugged me tightly and handed me a large bag of home-cooked goodies.

"Make sure you share and tell your friends hello." She wiped the tears off her cheek. "And don't worry. Brad will figure out something."

"Stay safe," I told her, then I followed Brad back

through my home hub towards the connecting tunnel. Brad was taking me back to the barricade where Mathew would meet me with a cart.

When I reached the tunnel, I found it hard to take the first step out of my hub. The smells, the sounds, and even the very air itself were a comfort to me. With the recent unrest in ECHO, I feared this might be the last time I would see my home.

But when Mathew waved at me from across the barricade, I took one last look at the odd, stacked houses in my hub and walked to the cart.

"How was your holiday?" Mathew asked with a smile.

"Good. Here, my grandmother wanted you to have this." I passed over a large parcel that held one of Mia's famous protein cakes. Mathew's smile spread as we traveled out to the main hub.

I knew the streets now. The road where the Pipe hub joined the main hub was well used. There were homes near the connecting tunnels and then a transition to apartment buildings. Next came several buildings with stores on their lower levels and dwellings above.

We had just passed the courtyard with the waterfall when a loud pop sounded somewhere from the back of the cart.

"What was that?" I asked as the cart gave a quick jerk to the right. I grabbed the dash, barely able to catch myself before I was thrown onto the sidewalk.

"I think one of the tires went flat," Mathew said as he jammed his foot on the brake. The cart rolled to a stop, and we were just disembarking when something large hit me from behind.

"Hey!" I heard Mathew shout as the floor rushed towards my face.

I didn't have time to put my hands out, and I hit the ground with my chin as a heavy weight landed on top of me.

"Get off him!" Mathew shouted, and I felt my arms being pulled back behind me.

It finally dawned on me that I was being attacked. I started to fight, but my arms had already been secured. Panic bloomed in me, and I kicked out with my legs. I heard a deep grunt and realized I knew the voice of my attacker. It was Gunny Brackson.

"Help!" Mathew finally shouted as I was picked up and thrown over Gunny's shoulder.

Blood from my chin ran down my face. I lifted my head and saw Mathew climbing over the disabled E-cart to give chase. Gunny was quicker and soon the bright courtyard gave way to a dark hallway followed by several stairs and then more darkness.

I continued to kick, but with my arms tied behind me, my struggle was in vain. Tears leaked out of my eyes and mixed with my blood as I started screaming.

I cussed and shouted as loud as I could as the large man easily carried me down into the bowels of the main hub. When we hit the first level, a glimmer of hope rose in me. I knew this tunnel. I hoped some of my fellow Pipers were near, and I doubled my efforts at kicking and yelling.

I was carried down two more levels before Gunny threw me on the ground. I hit my head again, but luckily my arms softened the blow. Bracing myself, I waited for whatever form of abuse the man would deliver. I was confused when I saw he wasn't even facing me.

In the faint light of the tunnel, I could see that his military hair cut was now grown out. He had a black eye, and his clothing was torn and tattered. His fists, which were raised, were bloodied and filthy.

"Before he comes, I need you to know," Gunny growled, casting a quick glance over his shoulder. "You need to know."

Shocked and a little dizzy from the blow to my head, I tried to make sense out of his words.

"She paid me. It wasn't my idea. I know what the reports say, but I had to tell someone. I know you will believe me. At least I hope you will." Gunny once again turned to face the dark tunnel beyond. "My kid can be a pain, but I would never seek revenge like that. I was paid."

"Paid?" I croaked; my throat raw from my screaming.

"Deller. She paid me to hurt you," Gunny said as he backed towards me, still facing the darkened tunnel we had just come from. "Follow the money and be careful," he warned as he turned and finally looked at me. "She's crazy."

With these last words, I heard a shout far down the tunnel. The noise indicated I was about to be rescued, and I turned in time to see Gunny Brackson flee in the opposite direction of my rescuers.

Chapter 15

Costs

For the next several days, all anyone could talk about was my abduction. I didn't tell anyone about Gunny's words, nor his implication that Joan Deller had paid him to attack me. But they wanted to hear, in detail, my daring escape from the dangerous Forcer.

I had already known Joan was evil. After all, I had witnessed her killing Hudson. I also knew she was sneaky, because she had posed as a recycling employee. With the news that she had hired Gunny to attack me, I feared for my life even more.

What would she do next? I needed to warn Adam Waltson. Maybe he could use his high position to... *To what?* I thought suddenly. I didn't know if they would send a woman like Deller to prison.

I told myself I needed to calm down. Brad had promised me he would send a warning to Adam. Maybe once Adam received the warning, he would know what to do.

There was a formal inquiry regarding my abduction a few days after I returned to school. Luckily, I didn't need to leave the Academy for this meeting, which was held in the dean's office. Only two council members were there, neither of which were Adam nor the Primary. They took my statement, during which I omitted Gunny's words of warning, and then they left.

A few days later I was awarded further funds on behalf of the Forcers' office. But it was only the news flash that came the next day that provided me with some relief.

The news stated that the Forcers' Master Commander was being held accountable for her failure in the hunt for Gunny Brackson. Also, they questioned the Master Commander's control of security of the hubs.

It appeared that several Primers were upset that a student had been abducted by the wanted ex-Forcer on their own streets and in their own hub. It wasn't mentioned that the student was a Piper, and mothers worried for their children while the wanted man was still at large.

The news article wasn't kind to the Forcers' office, and there were hints that a vote should be held to pick a new commander.

We had just returned from dinner, and I was checking the news to see if Gunny had been caught yet when a headline caught my eye. Evan glanced over at my screen.

"Word is, Omar is not returning to school," he said with a grim expression on his dark face.

"My mom's secretary is friends with Omar's grandmother, and it appears the family ran out of credits. They can't afford to send him back to school, so he's having to stay home," Rafe stated from his own cubby.

"What do you mean he's not coming back?" I asked. This news shocked me, and I felt a ball of ice form in the pit of my stomach.

"I guess they had a large amount of debt, and with Forcer Gunny gone..." Rafe replied.

"Good riddance to him," Evan said as he crossed his arms defiantly. "I hope they catch his dad soon. Crazy bunch, the whole lot, if you ask me."

"Debt? The Forcers didn't pay our reward, did they? I thought it was the Master Commander's office that paid us?" I asked.

"It was, but I think the two families were also charged. Something about work hazards," Rafe explained.

The ice in the middle of my gut now turned to nausea as Gunny's words came back to me. "Follow the money."

It was true, I didn't like Omar. He, Weston, and Manny had used every opportunity to bully me since I had first arrived at school and gotten between them and Breanna when they tried to bully her.

But it felt wrong to me that Omar couldn't return to school because of his father's actions. Especially since Gunny had abducted me only to warn me that he had been paid to attack me.

I didn't sleep well that night. The pain in my gut grew the more I thought about Omar's situation. I wondered what level he had been attempting to achieve. What limitations would he now have because of the actions of another? Would his life be difficult, much as mine had been because of my lack of parentage?

Suddenly the credits sitting in Mia's account didn't look so appealing. If the payments we received were causing another person hardship, I no longer wanted them.

About midnight I reached over and flipped my tablet on. I sent Mia a quick message and asked if Brad could find out some details for me. I wanted to know exactly where the funds had come from and what the status of the two Forcers' families was. If Gunny had been paid to attack me, maybe Forcer Simon would have as well.

When I was finished, I turned off the tablet and the ball of ice in my stomach melted a little. I wouldn't take another credit if it meant someone else would suffer.

An hour later I finally fell asleep. The dreams I had that night were of large credits chasing me and trying to eat me whole. I ran down the dark tunnels of the pipes to escape them only to stop when I reached the room where Hudson lay dying.

His last words were still echoing in my mind when the alarm sounded, waking me for school.

I spent all my free time the next several days searching for details about Forcer Gunny Brackson and his family. I learned that Omar, like many other Prime hub children, was an only child. His mother had worked when she was younger but stopped when she married Gunny.

Gunny had been a level six Forcer, which meant he could choose his base of operation. Up until the start of this school year, he had worked in the main hub's downtown station. There were twenty Forcers positioned there, in charge of a ten-block radius.

The family had lived in a flat along the edge of his patrol area. Since the incident, however, Omar's mother had moved them out of the apartment and back with her parents near the connecting tunnel between the Prime hub and the Printer hub.

My findings didn't include any information about her parents, nor if Omar was currently living there with her. I also couldn't find out if Omar would be restricted in employment based on his father's actions, so I set that aside for the time being.

As far as I knew, Omar might now receive the same type of treatment I had as a child, all because I didn't have a father. Scorn and ridicule had made me who I was today, but I had grown up with this treatment. Omar hadn't. I couldn't imagine living a normal life then one day having it all taken away.

I saw Weston and Manny in class every day, and part of me wanted to ask them about Omar. But the hateful looks they sent in my direction made it clear they would not be open to discussion.

I told my friends my misgivings, and they tried to reassure me that Omar and his mom wouldn't be treated badly based on Forcer Gunny's actions. But I didn't fully believe them.

Mia replied to my inquiry two days later stating that Brad had asked around, but the Forcers in the downtown station weren't willing to openly discuss a fellow Forcer's actions.

With limited information and the sour feeling in my gut, the weeks following my abduction seemed long. New Year's Day seemed forever away, despite it being on the upcoming Monday. Each hour felt like a day, and days felt like a week. I spent my time studying and sleeping, but nothing could drag me away from the sour mood I was in.

The previous year, Breanna's friend had asked us to her aunt's home for a celebration. But Breanna couldn't ask me this year, as she still wasn't allowed to be around me. The thought of spending New Year's Eve alone depressed me, but Miles and Evan came up with a plan.

"Look, my parents have to work that night, so they asked if I wanted to have you three over," Miles said, trying to look uninterested in our responses. "Mom said we can order whatever we want from the printer," he added, and I saw a glint of excitement in his eyes.

"I'll be there," Evan said, patting his rumbling stomach.

"Count me in too. Asher left for home today and won't

be back until later on the first," Rafe said with a grin.

"I guess I can go too," I said. Evan punched me in the arm, and I retaliated with my own. I missed his arm, and Evan laughed as he scooted out of reach.

New Year's Eve came, and my excitement grew. I hadn't seen Miles's home yet, nor Rafe's. Both of Miles's parents had treated my wounds previously, and I was looking forward to seeing what life in the medical half of the hub was like, especially for doctors.

The home Miles grew up in was across the dome from school. We rode our Z-riders over on Sunday evening with our overnight packs slung over our shoulders. The house was a standalone structure with a walkway on each side. It was three stories, and little green plants grew along short windows and the sidewalks.

"Mom likes to grow her own herbs," Miles said, and two patches of red covered his cheeks as he ducked his head and picked up his rider.

The home was neat and clean. The door opened into a small room where Miles said we could store our riders. Beyond that was a large living space that connected to the kitchen. It was the largest kitchen I had ever seen. Marble countertops reflected the glow of the overhead lights, and a large shiny printer stood in one corner. There was an eating nook, as Miles called it, which held a table and a bench.

He showed us the outside space just beyond the kitchen, a flat area right behind the house that had a bench and odd little instruments.

"Dad collects them," Miles said as Evan bent to look at one.

"Those are spindles!" Evan said with a smile. "I haven't

seen one before, but Dad told me about them."

"Yeah, they are really old," Miles said with a shrug. "They used to test the air, before ECHO."

"Test?" I asked, but Miles shrugged again.

"Don't ask me. They aren't functional. Dad just likes the way they look."

Next, Miles showed us his room up on the third level. He shared the floor with his mother's home office. Between the two rooms sat his own private bathroom.

We threw our overnight bags on his bed as Evan rubbed his stomach. "Where's the food?" he asked with a grin.

We ate cakes, protein links, a dish Miles called pizza, and a soft cold treat that tasted like pure sugar to me. Miles had several E-games, all linked to the large screen in the family room. We spent the entire evening playing these and didn't even realize the New Year had come as we laughed and joked.

When Miles's mother came home the next day, she discovered four sleeping boys lying in various angles all over her living room.

She made us home-cooked flat cakes and protein links and a big bowl of fruit orbs. We talked about the games we had played and school. Dr. Sanderson was easy to talk to, and she asked about the safety caps and our Z-rider productions.

When it came time to leave, we helped clean her front room and then packed up our things. However, before we could walk out the door, she pulled me aside.

"Zane," she said, and I saw a little worry in her eyes. "Please be safe," she said. I felt she wanted to tell me more, but Evan had just bumped up against me, and she quickly replaced the frown with a smile. "You boys all be safe. No more visits to the hospital!" she said as she waved us off.

Two weeks after New Year's, the hubs were shut down again. There was talk this time that the action was because of a march in the main hub, but no news was given either by the channels or school officials. I tried to ask Mia about the march and the status of the Pipe hub, but my communications weren't being opened. This concerned me, so I asked Rafe if he knew anything about it as we all settled down for schoolwork.

"I know there was something planned, but with us at school, we've left some of the EFAP stuff to Breanna's man." Rafe looked at me from his desk. "I did confirm that all the hubs are closed, but I think only for another day."

"Why does this keep happening?" I asked as Evan and Miles turned to look at us.

"I heard the Forcers are trying to track down the leader, but they won't find him, cause it's not one person," Evan said with a smile.

"Nope," Miles said. I saw a smile cross his face, and it was so uncharacteristic that I turned to look at my friend more closely.

"What do you mean?" I asked. Why were my friends taking the news of the hubs being shut down so easily?

"Well, there's more than one head to EFAP. They can track one, but they won't find them all." Miles shrugged his thin shoulders. "There's many now that even we don't know."

"That many?" I asked, turning back to Rafe.

"Word got out and the movement has grown," Rafe said as he turned back to his schoolwork. "Soon the Primary will realize she can't stop it."

"But it's not the Primary doing the closing. I heard it's mostly the Forcers' office," Evan said, and this news caused me to turn and study him.

"The... Master Commander?" I asked as fear and dread filled me.

"Yeah, she's making a power play. It appears she's been claiming that Primary Kasher isn't handling the whole thing and so she has taken over, at least when it comes to the EFAP marches," Evan supplied.

"Do you know if she'll win?" I asked as sweat started to form on my skin. If Joan gained control of the government, that would be bad.

"No. Despite the conflict right now, Forcers' MC can't gain a high position like the Primary," Rafe said with a shake of his head. "I think the worst that would happen is the committee would do a full review. Primary Kasher might face charges, but they won't ask her to step down."

"I heard no one really wants her job," Evan replied.

"I don't envy Breanna. When she has to take the job, the government might be in even worse condition," Miles said from his cubby.

I spent that night researching and discovered my friends were correct. The Master Commander position was at a much lower level than the Primary. I was filled with relief until I saw the powers Joan Deller had.

Under her position, she had full control of the Forcers. This included actions regarding each hub. When there were conflict actions in a hub, this gave the Master Commander full control of that hub, with some limitations. This is why the hubs would only be close to each other for another day. One of the limitations was a twenty-four-hour restriction. If it was proven the issue required clean-up time, then another twelve hours could be added.

Were all of these 'marches' giving Joan more control than she had previously had? I tried to find anything regarding the recent actions but couldn't find anything. I considered asking my friends again, but something stopped me.

I knew Rafe, Evan, and Miles had started the revolution with good intentions and a hope that they were making ECHO a better place for all, but something made me wonder. Were they really concerned about the Pipes? If so, wouldn't they be concerned about my home hub being closed so often? Couldn't they see that their actions, or the actions of EFAP, caused great distress for those they were trying to help?

I pondered this for several days and when my next tutoring lessons with Mitch happened, I had several questions for my friend. I had to wait until the others left that night and then I relayed my worries to him.

"I told you," Mitch said. "I knew nothing good would come from all this."

I was frustrated by his reaction. "That's not helping me." I stood from the table to pace a short path in his front room. "I'm worried. If Joan gets in control, that won't be good."

"She can't gain full control, but yeah, her shutting down the hubs isn't good." Mitch watched me pace. "We need to stop this club your friends have started."

"Mitch, I can't stop it. I don't even know who is involved. I haven't been included in anything. I think they know that, despite me initially wanting this, I wouldn't like what they are doing," I said, and my frustration grew even more. "I would never involve so many people. People I don't even know."

"You said Breanna and Mia's boyfriend are leading most of it. Can you talk to them?" Mitch urged. "Maybe get them to stop?"

Chapter 16

Secrets

I thought about Mitch's words that week. I knew I couldn't get in touch with Brad, but I was in the same room with Breanna every day. I hoped she would listen to my appeal to slow down the movement if I could somehow talk to her privately.

I couldn't approach her in class while the professors were watching, but maybe I could find a way to talk to her during mealtimes. I pondered this problem and finally came up with a solution. I would pass her a note asking her to meet me outside the kitchen hall during lunch break. This would give us more time and maybe a little privacy. There was a bench outside the back door that wasn't used by students much, so it might work.

I printed a note and hoped I would have a chance to pass it to her in our first class. She usually sat on the opposite side of the room, but if I caught her before she sat down, I could slip her the note.

I had no luck the first day, nor the second. However, on the third day, I made sure to leave breakfast early and had just settled outside the room when she came up with her friend Delany.

As she drew near me, I was able to slip her the note and then rush into the class to take my seat. I didn't even glance back to see if she'd read my message. I hoped she wouldn't read it right away and panicked when the professor entered the room right behind her. But when nothing was said, I took my tablet out and pretended to log on while my eyes remained locked on where Breanna sat.

That day, the morning lessons seemed to take forever. I wondered if Breanna would meet me, and I thought long and hard about what I was going to say to her.

When lunch finally came, I grabbed a pile of flat cakes and quickly turned towards the exit. The door wasn't near the main hall, so I kept looking over my shoulder in case someone followed me. I saw my friends looking around, but luckily, they hadn't seen me duck out of the hall towards the back doors.

Breanna wasn't there, and I felt my heart drop as I approached the empty bench. What if she didn't want to meet? What if she hadn't read my note? These thoughts filled my brain and made me panic as I glanced around.

"Over here," I heard Breanna hiss, and then I saw her head disappear behind a corner of the building.

She had hidden in a little inlet in the back wall of the building, away from the door. She looked worried and kept glancing around as I approached.

"Breanna." I stopped when she held a hand up.

"I can't stay long. Mom has my lunch period monitored, but Z, I know what you're going to say." She looked up at me.

It was the first time since school had started that I had seen her this close. I noticed she had worrying lines around her eyes and then remembered suddenly how pretty she was.

"Z, I can't stop what is happening right now. I know you think I should, but even the man in the main hub thinks this type of action has to continue."

"How did you know what I was going to ask you?" I demanded, taking a step closer.

"Oh, Z, Rafe told me. We have a class together. My mother thinks he's a good influence and has actually insisted I sit next to him. I think Mom is hoping we will start dating." Breanna shook her head. "But he's like a brother to me, always has been. Mom doesn't understand and so I've been utilizing this contact so Rafe and I can communicate and make plans for the revolution."

"Why can't you stop the marches, or at least slow it down? Too much is happening, and it's affecting my hub," I demanded.

"First, I don't want it to stop." A little frown appeared on her lips. "Second, we've made progress. Actual progress. The Prime Committee is now discussing new policies regarding the Pipes, policies that will help your hub."

"Like what?" I insisted.

"Well, there's talk that the Pipe hub will no longer be charged for the parts needed to do repairs. That's a huge step, one that wouldn't have been discussed prior to the marches. And then there's the increase in pay," she explained. "Though that one was vetoed during the last meeting."

"How do you know?" I asked, wondering how she knew so many details about the Prime committees' actions.

"Rafe's grandfather told me," Breanna said with a frown. "He's on the committee and also part of the revolution."

"Adam! You've talked with Adam Waltson?" I demanded.

"I can't tell you everything right now, we don't have time. Ask Rafe. He knows what he can tell you." She moved to leave. When I reached out and caught her arm, she turned back and sighed. "I'm glad you weren't hurt the other day." She reached up and placed a soft kiss on my cheek. I released her arm in shock, and she turned and bolted back into the building.

As I brushed a finger over my tingling cheek, I had the sudden urge to shout with joy, then I remembered her words. *"Rafe knows what he can tell you."*

So, my friends were keeping secrets from me, I thought with a sudden pang of suspicion. Didn't they trust me? Hurt by these thoughts, I stood outside the kitchen hall and pondered my friendships.

The more I thought about it, the angrier I became at the possibility that they were keeping things from me. Then I remembered I was keeping secrets from them as well. Dark, dangerous secrets. Ones I feared could destroy our friendship and possibly my life.

Did I trust Rafe, Evan, and Miles?

I closed my eyes, realizing I did trust them, completely. So what was keeping me from telling them everything?

Mia had told Brad Carrington our secret. She had trusted him enough that she had told him all about me witnessing the death of Hudson Adamson. She had even told him who the murderer was. The fact that it was the man's boss hadn't deterred my grandmother from telling him.

So why did I keep these facts from my best friends? People, I now realized, I trusted with my very life.

I understood, as I walked back to the hall, that it wasn't

a lack of trust that had kept me from telling them. It was the fact that it was Rafe's father who had died that kept me from speaking. I had no idea how Rafe would react to my secret, and it had prevented me from speaking about it all these months. Even now, it was his reaction alone that kept me from speaking up.

As I sat at the table, talk continuing around me, I realized I had to tell Rafe, no matter his reaction. I had to tell my secrets.

Tonight, I vowed I would tell him about his father.

Before bed that night, my palms grew damp with sweat, and I was twitchy with nerves. Miles asked me at dinner if I was ill, but he must have believed my excuse of jitters about a pending exam because he didn't ask me again.

When we arrived at our dorm room after the meal, I couldn't justify delaying anymore. After everyone had sat to finish various school assignments, I locked the door. I turned on the small music pod and asked them to join me in my cubby. I was worried we might be overheard by someone walking down the hall. The dorm building's walls weren't very thick, and I couldn't afford to have anyone overhear my conversation.

"I need to tell you something," I said. I pulled a chair out of Evan's space and pushed it towards Rafe, then sat on my own bed in front of him.

"Hey, if it's about your meeting with Breanna for a little kissing earlier, we already know," Evan said with a laugh.

"What?" I asked, shocked.

"Dude, it was written all over your face when you came back to lunch." He laughed and mimicked me rubbing a hand over my cheek with a goofy expression on his face.

"You kept rubbing a spot on your cheek and your face was bright red!" Rafe said with a laugh.

"No. I mean, you could tell?" I asked, my voice cracking. My face warmed as they all laughed at me again.

"About time," Miles mumbled as I sat there in shock.

"It's not about that." Shaking my head, I turned my eyes back to Rafe and took a deep breath. "Rafe, I need to talk to you about your dad."

The smile fell from Rafe's face, and his brows drew together in confusion. "What about my dad?"

I had thought about how I would start, but when it came down to it, I knew it would always start with Hudson's death.

"I was there," I blurted out, forgetting my plan to build up to the death in a long and gentle story. "I was there the night he was killed."

Silence fell suddenly in our room, and the only sound was the radio music blasting out of the speaker.

"What?" Evan hissed as Rafe finally sat in the chair and stared at me.

"I told you I had been traveling down in the Pipes for years. Well, the night your father died was the last night I went down in the tunnels alone. A friend had told me about a hidden control room. I went there to search for it and heard your dad coming. I didn't know who it was, so I hid. I would have gotten into trouble if I had been discovered down there, so I hid." I realized I had forgotten to breathe, so I paused and took a deep breath, then licked my lips before I continued. "He was arguing with a woman. They had started to leave the room that I was hiding in when she killed him." I felt my tears start to fall and tried to wipe them off my face, but the look of shock in Rafe's eyes kept me going. "I didn't know what the sound was. I had never heard a blast gun before." I felt Miles sit on the bed behind me as I continued.

"I found him afterwards." There was a pause in the music, so I stopped and waited for it to continue before I resumed my story. "He was still alive."

"Zap," I heard Evan hiss quietly.

"He was bleeding." My voice caught, and I had to take another breath before I went on. "He asked me to find Waltson. I didn't know who that was, but he wanted me to find him. He wanted me to tell Waltson he was sorry."

Miles's hand patted my back, which caused more tears to fall down my face. I never knew a kind and simple gesture could affect me so much. My voice left me, and I could no longer speak as my shoulders shook.

It wasn't until two songs later on the radio that Rafe finally spoke up. "Dad and Grandpa had fought the week before," he said as I looked up at him through my tears. "Dad wouldn't tell me what their fight was about, but it was a bad one."

I nodded, though I didn't really understand why. Then I wiped my face again and slowly continued. "I know now who killed him."

With these words Miles and Evan jumped up and started blasting questions at me, but Rafe remained seated.

"Tell me," was all he calmly said.

I told him everything. I explained my run-in with Joan Deller in the recycling piles, about my mysterious meeting with Adam in the Fixer hub, the night I was convinced I had been shot at. I even spoke about Gunny's words the day he had abducted me.

"You think Master Commander Deller killed Rafe's father and has paid to have you injured or even killed? Do you think she knows it was you down in the Pipes that night?" Evan asked with shock in his voice, which made it several octaves higher than usual.

I shrugged, then nodded and kept my eyes on Rafe. I had to tell him everything. Even things I wasn't a hundred percent sure of.

"I think she knows it's either me or my friend Mitch. He is the one who drew me the map to that room, a map I dropped and left near your father's body."

"But why would she pay someone to attack you?" Miles asked. "And why kill Rafe's dad?"

"I don't know." I took another deep breath before I spoke of my theories. "But I'm pretty sure my unknown school donor is Adam Waltson."

"Grandpa?" Rafe asked. He leaned back and looked at me with speculation. "Why? Why would Grandpa pay for your schooling?"

I shook my head and asked one of my own questions. "Why is your grandpa involved in the revolution?"

Rafe shrugged his shoulders and sighed. "Grandpa's always been an odd one. He's spoken up several times in the past about equality."

"Z, do you personally know Rafe's grandpa?" Evan asked.

"I met him once before I got the donation." I thought back to the time I met Adam in my home hub. "He said he knew my grandmother, but when I asked her, she didn't remember him."

"So why would he pay for your education?" Miles asked. "Do you think he knows you were there when his son died?"

"I don't think so. Only Mia, Mitch and I knew at that time," I replied. "Now you three know too."

"So, this Master Commander, the one that paid Gunny

to hurt you, do you think she was trying to kill you?" Evan asked.

"She's killed before." I scrunched my shoulders again.

"Why did she kill my dad?" Rafe asked quietly.

"He didn't want to give her time," I explained and then repeated the words I had heard over a year ago.

"She doesn't own him?" Rafe mumbled as he finally stood and walked over to turn the music up louder so it would cover our voices in case someone was listening.

"What does that mean?" Evan asked.

"I heard Grandpa say something similar last holiday." Rafe turned to study me. "Secrets," he mumbled. "She knew his secrets."

"What was your father doing in the tunnels?" Miles interjected finally as we all looked at Rafe.

"Probably the same thing Grandpa does in them," Rafe replied with a shrug. "I was supposed to shadow Dad last summer, but his death prevented it. Before that, he had me fitted for a chest plate, and I remember he insisted it have the colors of every level. I thought it was strange at the time, but Dad said sometimes his work took him to the other hubs. He told me he found it useful to have multiple colors. It caused fewer questions."

"What kind of work took him down into the Pipes?" I asked.

Another shrug from Rafe left me frustrated until he walked over to his own cubby and said, "I don't know, but I can ask Grandpa."

Fear and panic set in as Rafe moved to open his tablet. "No." I quickly moved to stop him. "Not yet. There's more I need to tell you."

I told them of Mitch's warnings, about the danger we could be in if Joan had any idea how much I knew. I talked about the revolution and asked how deeply Adam was involved.

"He's funding it," Rafe said. "Breanna can't get any help from her mother, but Brad and a few of his friends were willing to help. But money was needed and since Grandpa's always been for equality, I asked him."

"He's paying for all of it?" I asked, shocked.

"Well, yeah," Rafe said with a smile.

"Brad said he had a way to warn Adam about Joan," I provided. "But I worry all these marches are putting my home hub in danger."

"The lockdowns," Evan mumbled with a nod.

"I worry it's giving Joan more power. And it's putting too much pressure on the Pipers," I said as I sat back down on my bed.

"Don't you see, it's also doing some good," Rafe exclaimed.

"I know. Breanna told me about some of the ideas up for votes right now, but you guys aren't there. You didn't see my hub during a lockdown."

"Well, that's a great idea," Miles said with a smile.

Chapter 17

Time

Every night after my confession, my friends talked about the revolution. Evan suggested we have a sit-in, an event where supporters march to the Pipe hub and block the entrance to support those who were locked inside.

I was able to talk him out of this. I voiced my concerns that the hub would be locked and closed permanently. After hearing my fears, he agreed to table this idea until later.

Rafe wanted to ask his grandfather his opinion and also tell him about my secrets, but I talked him out of that as well. My fear that Joan would strike out against me, or my family again, was so strong that I'm sure my friends heard the fear in my voice.

In the end, they agreed they would let Brad send his message of warning to Adam and do nothing until then. They only agreed to this when I vowed that I would stop trying to pressure them into halting the revolution. I had to trust that these marches were getting some good results.

Terraform day was fast approaching and that meant

quarterly finals. My struggles with grades still kept me busy most nights, though my study sessions with Mitch helped raise some of my grades.

Mitch was shocked and concerned when I found time to tell him about my confessions to my bunk mates. Mitch worried that Rafe would blab to his grandfather, but I told Mitch that, at this point, I wasn't convinced it would be a bad thing.

"If Waltson knows, then maybe I won't have to fear Joan Deller. Maybe he'd take care of her for me," I hissed. I crossed my arms and leaned back from the large table in his room.

"But what if he can't deal with her?" Mitch asked with a shake of his head. "What if she knows *his secrets?*"

"Mitch, I don't think Waltson is scared of anyone." I tried to think back to his words that I had overheard in the hospital after my injuries at the start of the year.

"No one will dare attack one that holds my name." I didn't quite understand this statement, but I remembered Adam's voice had been filled with conviction.

Mitch wasn't convinced and eventually some of his worry rubbed off on me. I remained vigilant every day and traveled with my friends or walked in large groups of people. I never walked alone.

When tests were done and Terraform day was upon us, my excitement grew. I was looking forward to seeing Mia and even Brad again. I hoped Brad would provide me with details about his idea to inform Adam of the dangers.

Evan and Rafe hoped to travel to my home during the holiday break, since all restrictions had been lifted. My anticipation of the holiday increased, and we made plans to fill our time together with fun and exploration.

Mathew Carlson arrived on the first day of the break

and drove me home. The border barrier was missing this time, so he was able to drive the cart all the way into the hub.

I was excited and shocked to see several differences inside my home. The first thing I noticed was the air. Fresh air blasted across my face as Mathew parked the cart. My home hub still smelled of cooked spices, but the stale musty stench was missing.

The second thing I noticed was that the burned-out bulbs had finally been replaced. Raising my eyebrows, I turned and studied the homes nearest the connecting tunnel. When I didn't notice any physical difference there, I bent and picked up my bag.

"I can walk home from here, sir." I waved Mathew off then quickly jogged home.

Mia was there, but Brad was at work. She told me that he would be joining us for dinner the next night. She clarified that Brad wanted to explain things to me himself regarding his contact with Waltson.

"Stop nagging. I promised Brad that I would let him explain it all to you." Mia frowned at me. "I think I need to let out your pants an inch or two. You've grown again," she clucked. She grabbed her measuring tape and a jug of pins.

Restless and annoyed after dinner, I told Mia I was going over to see Mitch, but she worried about me walking so close to bedtime when the lights were dim in our hub. I agreed I would wait until the next day. After all, I didn't want to get abducted or attacked again. Even though I was in my home hub, it didn't mean I was safe.

Early the next morning, I jogged over to Mitch's home only to discover that he and his mother had gone out. I didn't see them on the path on my way back home, so I sent a quick message to Mitch's tablet asking if we could meet after lunch. It was rare for us to spend time together, unless we were working on school studies, and I had so much to tell him.

An hour after returning home, I got a message from Mitch that he could meet me at our usual spot near the hub wall.

"I have loads to tell you," he wrote, which piqued my interest.

The hours seemed to stretch before I could leave to meet Mitch. I spent the time getting fitted for new shirts and pants. Mia wanted to fit me for new shoes too, but I told her I would stop and get some in the main hub on my way back to school.

She frowned for a minute then nodded in agreement. "I guess we can afford to spend credits. Just make sure you get them slightly larger than you need so your feet have room to grow."

When lunch was finished and it was finally time to leave, I loaded up a newly made two-way talker for Mitch that I had built the night before and made my way to our meeting spot.

When Mitch arrived, his cheeks were flushed, and he had a big smile on his face.

"Zane, you'll never guess!" he exclaimed as he wobbled over to me. I bent down to tweak the length of his crutches as he talked. "Mom and I met with Advisor Jeffson this morning, that's where we were when you stopped by," Mitch said as I found the right height for his crutch.

"Oh?" I mumbled.

"He said he is interested in sending another Piper to the Academy!" Mitch exclaimed. He grabbed my arm as I stood up. "I get to read the application essays and decide who will go, but our hub will actually pay for a student to go to the Academy!"

"What?" My mouth dropped open with awe.

"I guess he's looking for more administrative assistants and since you and I turned him down, he ran the numbers and said that our hub can now afford to send one student per year to school."

A frown appeared on Mitch's face as I stood there with my eyes wide with shock at this news.

"I don't know if it will be different students each year for only a level one, but Zane, this is progress!" Mitch smiled. "Think about it. Some kids will break free from the Pipes and get the opportunity to have a safe job. Some family can rest easy knowing their child has a chance at a high-paying job, one that's safe."

"When did Advisor Jeffson want to start?" I asked. "Is he thinking of next school year?"

"He was hoping the school would match our hub's fees and maybe two students could go, but at this point the funds will be ready by next school year. But we have to encourage families to have their children submit an essay." Mitch frowned and a worried look crossed his face before he continued. "Of course, we also have to ensure there are no cheaters."

"You'll figure something out," I said with a smile. It quickly dropped away when the ground shook and a loud booming noise rocked the entire hub.

Concerned that Mitch would be thrown off his feet, I reached forward and grabbed his arms as his crutches fell to the hard floor. Another boom came, followed by another tremor as dust and dirt fell down on us from the dome's ceiling.

When the shaking stopped, the sounds of the fire alarms

rang out. Bending quickly, I grabbed Mitch's crutches and thrust them at him. Then I raced down the walkway towards the smoke and screams.

The smell of smoke permeated the entire hub. It burned my lungs as I raced towards the heat and confusion. I could hear screams and someone excessively sobbing, and my heart raced in my ears.

Before I neared the fire, I knew there weren't going to be any survivors. The entire block where Mitch's home had once stood was now a crater of rubble and flames. Burned metal and fire whirled around the area as people scrambled back from the carnage.

The explosion had been proficient and the results deadly. People were rushing forward with buckets of water while others walked around in a daze, their clothing black and their faces wide with shock. I saw an elderly woman stumble past me and realized I didn't even recognize her through all the soot and blood.

I heard the sound of Mitch's crutches hitting the ground behind me and whirled around to block my friend from the horrific sight.

"No," I croaked, grabbing his arms. "There's nothing you can do."

Mitch's face was pale, his eyes wide and already filled with tears as he gazed over my shoulder. He shook his head once as the alarms in the hub kept up their high-pitched screaming.

Someone bumped past us, and I felt the real danger he and I were in for the first time since the bomb had exploded.

"Mitch, we have to get out of here!" I pushed him back

the way we had come. I bent and grabbed his cane then dragged my small friend down a narrow walkway.

I was filled with fear for not only me and Mitch, but for Mia as well. As I struggled with the limp form of my friend, my panicked mind raced with possibilities of danger. Was she next? Was my own home a target too?

"Mitch, I have to check on Mia!" I hissed, half expecting another loud boom at any moment. He nodded once, but his eyes were still glazed as I helped him sit on a step near the back wall of the dome.

"Stay here. I'll run and get her, then we're all getting out of here." To ensure he stayed put, I kept his crutches in my hands as I whirled around and raced home.

The sound of the fire suppressant system and the alarms rang in my ears as I rushed past people heading towards the disaster. Everyone had concern and fear on their faces, causing me to increase my pace.

Two alleyways away from my home, a large hand grabbed my arm, and I was yanked sideways. I swung out with Mitch's crutches and took satisfaction from the loud 'crack' and the grunt that followed.

"Get off me!" I screamed before a hand clamped firmly over my mouth.

"Shh," Brad growled as Mia rushed forward and hugged me.

"Oh, Zane!" she sobbed as I dropped the crutches and wrapped my arms around her.

"Quickly, we need to get out of here before they lock down the tunnel," Brad warned as he rubbed his shoulder where I had hit him.

"Mitch!" I exclaimed, grabbing the fallen crutches. "He's over against the wall. We have to bring him!"

Brad nodded once and peeked out of the walkway.

"Quickly, lead the way, but stay off the main walkways," he urged as we headed back towards where I had left my friend.

Mitch was still sitting on the step, but his tears had stopped falling as he sat there, his eyes glassy with shock as his body shook.

"Oh dear," Mia exclaimed as she wrapped her shawl around the boy's shoulders.

"Here, I'll carry him." Brad picked Mitch up and then motioned with his chin. "Zane, take the lead. Quickly, head to the connection tunnel."

As we hurried down the narrow ways of my home hub, I felt the teeth of danger nipping at our heels. Every corner now hid dangers, each person running past was now an enemy. Every breath seemed to scream at me that it might be my last.

The connecting tunnel hadn't yet been closed, but as we made it out into the main hub and headed down a side street, we heard the sirens of the Forcers heading towards the Pipe hub.

"They will probably close the streets here too. If we hurry, we can make it to my place first," Brad urged as he led the way.

Brad's home was a little two-room apartment three blocks from where we had first met him over a year before. It sat six stories up and was clean but didn't have much furniture in it. Both bedrooms had a bed, and he had one chair with a small table for eating near the kitchen.

Mia immediately set about making some tea for Mitch, who still hadn't spoken a word. I went into the bathroom and wiped the soot off my face, then brought a wet cloth and gave it to Mitch. When he made no move to take it, I washed the grime off his hands and face.

"We need to keep him warm," Mia said as she laid a blanket over Mitch's small legs.

"I'll get it dirty," Mitch croaked as he tried to lift the blanket off his spoiled clothes.

"Don't worry about that, love. The dirt will wash off," Mia crooned, running a hand down Mitch's head.

"I need to go to work. I can let them know Mitch is alive and find out any other details about his family," Brad said as he came out of his room dressed in his uniform. "Stay here and don't answer the door, no matter who they say they are," he warned as he placed a kiss on Mia's lips.

When Mia placed the tea on the small table near the sofa, I noticed her hands were shaking. She walked back into the kitchenette and came back with a small plate of cookie orbs.

Mitch's shock wore off an hour later. His body shook from his sobs, and Mia held him tight as he cried. He had confirmed that his entire family had been home when he left the house to meet me.

"They were all there. We were getting ready for the feast, but I wanted to tell Zane the news." He sobbed as I watched from across the room while Mia comforted him.

"There, there," Mia soothed as she ran a hand over his head. "We will wait until Brad comes home; he will have news of your family."

But Brad didn't come home that night. I slept in the spare bed with Mitch while Mia stayed on the couch. Mitch didn't sleep much, but sometime around midnight his sobs stopped.

The next day Mia had a warm breakfast waiting for us. Her eyes were red, and worry lines etched on her face as she served us the food. Mitch didn't want to eat anything, but Mia urged him to eat a little. We had turned on the news reports, trying to find out more details about the explosion and fire, but the news upset Mitch, so Mia quickly turned it off again.

When Brad finally arrived, it was with the dreaded news we had all feared. Mitch's mother, father, two brothers, and three sisters were all dead.

Chapter 18

News

In total, twelve people had died when the bombs ripped through the hodgepodge homes built of scrap metal.

Forcers and inspectors had arrived and taken over the scene. As Brad had feared, the tunnel into the Pipe hub had been blocked and only the emergency crews were allowed in or out.

Brad informed us he had been allowed back into the hub and had assisted in putting the fire out. A total of three homes had been demolished by the explosion, while four more structures had suffered major fire damage. Most of the hub's lights had been broken in the explosion and fire suppressant now covered the entire hub, thanks to the working suppressant pipes along the dome's ceiling.

"You'll stay with me until you go back to school in two days, then I will see if guards can be detailed to you both," Brad said as he took a sip of the tea Mia had made him. "I don't care what the dean says, you two are no longer safe."

"I'm not going back," Mitch hissed as he wiped the tears from his face.

"Nonsense," Mia said. She grabbed his hand and squeezed it. "You have to think of your future. Your family would want you to continue with your education."

Despite the reassurances, Mitch remained firm in his commitment to never return to the Academy. But the next day, we had an unexpected visitor.

Primary Kasher and her advisor Davis Elliotson knocked on Brad's door shortly after ten in the morning. The Primary's face was sober, her eyes filled with concern as she asked to speak with Mitch.

"I'm sorry, Primary, I don't think he is ready for any visitors," Mia apologized, but then Mitch came into the room from the back bedroom.

"I'm here," Mitch said as he studied the Primary with red eyes. He sat on the nearest chair, and Primary Kasher walked over and knelt in front of him.

"Mitch." She placed a hand on his shoulder as she studied him. "I am so sorry for your loss."

Mitch took a deep breath, and I knew he was fighting back his tears again.

"I have talked to all of the victims' families," Kasher started, sitting on the chair next to Mitch's. "But you are the sole survivor of your family." She paused here as Mia rushed over and stood behind Mitch.

"He is not alone," Mia said sternly.

"Of course not," Kasher said with a nod. "However, since Mitch and I are acquainted, I thought it best to file for guardianship." Kasher turned back to Mitch and studied him. "You know Breanna, my daughter. Well, I have a large place and have started preparations for a room for you. This way you have a safe place to stay when school is out."

"You want him to live with you?" I asked. All eyes turned to me.

"There are reasons why this would be a good idea, besides his safety," Kasher said with a frown. "And the Prime Committee agreed. They have already granted my guardianship."

"So, he doesn't have a choice?" I demanded. Mia took a sharp breath in, indicating she disapproved of my harsh words spoken to the Primary of ECHO.

"Zane," Mia scolded, but she stopped when Kasher held her hand up.

"No, it's quite all right. Zane and I don't have the best history. But Mitch does have a choice. I'm here to ask if he would like to come and live with me." Kasher leaned towards Mitch who sat quietly in his chair.

"You would be safe and have anything you could wish for if you were to join the Primary," Davis Elliotson said as he stood in the doorway.

The Primary and her advisor left only when Mitch promised to think about the offer. Mia asked me to remain quiet about my opinions, as this was a discission Mitch would have to make by himself.

When we left for school two days later, there were still no new details about the cause of the fire. Only the total dead had been given, but that didn't include names or ages of the deceased.

Since Mathew didn't know where I had moved to, Brad contacted the Academy and told them he would be driving Mitch and I back to the school.

When we got to the Academy, Brad introduced us to the guards the school had hired. My assigned guard, Tim Cloudson, was as big as Brad but sported a bald head and a thick mustache. Mitch was assigned a mixed-raced man named Ryan Flintson. Both guards studied us as they explained that we weren't going anywhere without them.

Ryan helped Mitch to his rooms while Tim and I walked into the dorm building.

"I've been given the room at the front of the hallway on your floor, so no one can get to you unless they pass me," he growled. I tried to picture the large man sitting in all my classes.

When lessons started the next day, the buzz around school was the bombing. Despite the news channels not releasing much information, the students had a lot to discuss.

There was speculation that the whole Pipe hub had collapsed and rumors that half the hub was now under rubble. Another story said that a gang from the resistance had set the bomb off to get sympathy for the Pipers, a publicity stunt in an attempt to further their cause. This was quickly squelched, as no one believed it, but I was amazed at how many stories were spreading. Everyone had a theory, and they all seemed eager and willing to spread their own ideas.

When I showed up to class, I was immediately surrounded by students wanting to know what had happened. After two days of questions, to which I had no answers, the students lost interest in me.

Two weeks after the explosion, a death ceremony was held for Mitch's family. I was allowed to attend, but Mia and Brad thought it was too risky, so I remained at school instead. I saw clips of the ceremony and raised my eyebrows when a video of Mitch walking next to Primary Kasher flashed on the screen. Kasher had her hand on one of Mitch's shoulders as they walked towards a tall black building.

The news reporters all speculated that Mitch would be living with the Primary after school was finished for the year. They made it sound as if Kasher was a hero for offering to take in the "poor crippled orphan." I cringed when I heard those words used to describe Mitch.

When Mitch returned to school the next day, most pupils seemed to respect his situation. No one voiced anything but sorrow and sympathy. Two nights later, when Mitch resumed study club, I was able to speak with him alone.

"Have you heard anything from Brad or the inspectors?" I asked, frustrated at having to wait so long to finally speak with my friend.

"They know it was a bomb. The inspector met with me a week ago and asked me about my house. He wanted to know if Mom or Dad kept anything illegal in our home," Mitch hissed as he leaned closer. His once-youthful face now seemed older. There were lines around his eyes and a permanent one between his brows. "He kept asking, and when I finally told him a firm no, my parents didn't keep explosives in our home, he told me they had found an unexploded device. There had been three total, but only two detonated."

"Zap," I said, shaking my head in shock.

"Zane, if all three had gone off, half the hub could have gone up in smoke that day." Mitch's voice cracked a little.

"You were with me," I whispered. "You're safe. *We're* safe now." I turned to see our guards, Tim and Ryan, standing near the doorway to Mitch's rooms.

"Zane, two nights ago they finally found my family." Mitch leaned closer to me. "The inspector told me they also found the body of Forcer Gunny Brackson in the wreckage."

. . .

Three days later, the news channels finally released the information regarding Forcer Gunny's body being discovered in the rubble of the explosion. The announcers speculated that it had been the dead man who had set the bombs, but I had my doubts.

If he had intended to harm or kill, then why had he released me all those days ago? Why had he warned me about Master Commander Joan? Why hadn't he just killed me?

Somehow the death of Gunny made me even more fearful of Joan. I knew she was capable of murder and had a theory she had killed Forcer Simon Woodson after the horrible results at the beginning of the school year. I believed she had even taken a shot at me before school in the Fixer hub.

Now I pondered the possibility that she had blown up the homes in the Pipe hub, homes with children in them. Mia and Brad doubted my theory, but Rafe, Evan, and Miles agreed with my guess.

My birthday had come and gone, and I was sixteen. The new disc I had gotten from Evan was tossed back to me as we discussed the events of the last month.

"If she killed my dad, she definitely could have blown up Mitch's home. After all, she knew it was his map found near my dad," Rafe stated as his eyes narrowed with anger.

"Aren't you worried she'll come after you next?" Miles asked, his usually sober eyes round with shock.

"Brad thinks she can't. At least not while I'm at school and guarded. Even Mitch should be safe here. That's why the Primary has him stay with her after school. Brad thinks Kasher knows Mitch would be in more danger if he were to live anywhere else," I replied.

"But what about you?" Evan demanded as he tossed the

disc to me outside our dorm building. My guard and permanent shadow, Tim, was sitting on the bench a few feet away.

"I'll be going back to live with Brad. Mia has already moved most of our stuff there. His building has good security and, well, he's a Forcer."

Our talk turned to grades and girls, which always came next, but we still pondered the unbelievable events that had orphaned Mitch and locked down the Pipe hub for three whole weeks after the bombing.

The EFAP had taken a break after the bombing. Breanna had worried the news would hint the revolutionaries were responsible, so she had called a halt, and Brad had been quick to agree with her. All marches had stopped, and things had grown quiet regarding the revolution. Yet the first victory had already been won. The Pipers were now receiving two new benefits. All parts were now being charged to the Primary hub, and work had already started to improve the living arrangements in the Pipe hub. Of course, repairs had started in the damaged blocks. A vote had been taken, and the Pipers didn't want to replace the homes. They insisted an open space be left there, and a memorial would be opened two weeks after school was finished.

The end of the school year was around the corner, and we took a break from our studies for the first time in ages. Rafe caught the disc as he continued to speculate about the outcome in a quiet tone. "If Deller set the bombs, there's got to be some proof she did it."

"My dad said he heard there were parts from the Fixer hub in the unexploded bomb," Evan said as he walked closer to catch the disc Rafe had thrown.

"What?" I asked quickly. I had a vision of the first time I had seen Joan standing in overalls.

"I guess almost everything has parts from the Fixer hub,

or the Printers. But Dad says the main components were from the Fixers. We have about twenty people who specialize in chemicals that can be used to clean, break down, and even dissolve things," Evan said with a shake of his head as he tossed the disc back to me.

"What else was used?" I asked, remembering what the aftereffect of the bombs looked and smelled like.

"I don't know. Dad won't tell me much more, but I'm guessing it took a lot of knowledge to build them." Evan cast a look over at my guard Tim to ensure he wasn't listening.

"Skill and material," Rafe mumbled. He was deep in thought, and he missed the disc that had been thrown at him.

"Well, Joan could have someone helping her," Miles speculated quietly.

"Or she could be blackmailing someone," Evan said as he moved to pick up the fallen disc.

"Blackmailing?" I asked, and something clicked into place. "She said, you know the night she killed Hudson, that he was no longer useful."

"You think she was blackmailing my dad?" Rafe asked.

I replied with a shrug. I honestly didn't know anything about Rafe's dad other than the intimate details of his death. "He said she didn't own him, that she owned others but not him." I turned to look at Rafe again. "No, I don't think she was blackmailing him. But maybe Evan is correct. Maybe she's not working alone."

"So how do we go about finding this out?" Miles demanded.

Suddenly I was grateful for my friends. I was no longer alone in my worries and dark thoughts of Hudson's death. Even my concerns about his killer were no longer my own. I had friends, a support group, and they were just as worried as I had been since that fateful night down in the Pipe tunnels so long ago.

"I might have a way, but after the bombing, we all need to be careful," Rafe insisted. "Let me think about it for a while."

The day before finals came and with it my nerves. I was worried about my programing grade and had used my study times with Miles to understand the recent diagram the professor had assigned us.

Mitch told me he wasn't looking forward to moving into the Primary's home. He missed his family and often talked to me about them. Every conversation resulted in tears, and I would comfort him as best I could.

When Mitch spoke of moving in with Kasher and Breanna, he worried about being secluded. "I don't suppose you could get the TWT working again?" he asked the last night before finals.

"I forgot!" I exclaimed and slapped a hand on my forehead. "I totally forgot I already built them. I had them with me when, well..." I fell silent, and Mitch nodded in understanding. "I can bring them tomorrow. After all, we will be in the same hub and can use them to speak every night like we used to."

"I keep forgetting you are going to be living in the Prime hub too," Mitch said with a frown. "But aren't you spending most of your time in the Fixer hub working on your Z-riders?"

"Yeah, but I'm spending my first week with Mia. Her wedding is the day after the level ceremony." I frowned and added, "I hope I pass."

"You will. You just need to study harder," Mitch said with a shrug of his shoulders.

Chapter 19

Finals

The fifth month of the year came swiftly, and with it came finals for my level two.

Students had stopped playing or goofing off between classes and now spent their time memorizing lessons. Everywhere I went there were kids with their noses plastered against their tablets, trying to get a few more minutes of lessons in before finals.

Mitch increased his study sessions and now had four more students coming each night. I had joined his other two sessions and was trying to increase my knowledge of the lessons in accounting and programing.

Even Evan, who usually appeared carefree, was seen bent over a nasty diagram of wires one night as he mumbled about currents and power voltage.

The night before my government test, I had a nasty dream that Primary Kasher came to personally tell me my test scores were so bad that she was there to take away my level one standing.

I somehow made it through the tests for base class and

government class, which left four more tests. The tests were so long that this year they conducted only two tests per day.

Two classes actually required a written and an exercise test. I wasn't worried about my mechanics finals. That was the class I had my best grades in.

The class finale I was most worried about was programing. Not the exercise, as I had done enough inventing and building to assist with this portion of the test. No, it was the long diagrams and written essay that had me sweating through the entire three hours.

When the test was finally over, I was too tired to think about going for dinner, but Evan and Miles insisted on dragging me there to meet Rafe and a few others.

"Look, your last finals are tomorrow. No more studying," Evan insisted as he tugged me off my bunk and out our dorm door. "Tonight, we eat!"

Tim Cloudson was standing outside the main door when we came out and headed to the kitchen hall. I had gotten so used to the large guard being near me that I barely registered his presence unless he spoke.

As we neared the hall, I was reminded he was there when he thrust one of his hands out and stopped me from entering behind my friends.

"Trouble," Tim said as I looked up at him with shock on my face. "Over there." He placed a hand on my forearm.

I followed his gaze and saw Weston and Manny standing a few feet from the door. Both boys were glancing at me and for once Manny wasn't wearing a stupid smile on his face. Neither seemed to be glowering at me, but they didn't appear to be happy either.

I had a quick uncomfortable feeling, but it wasn't concern or worry for my safety. Instead, I thought of their friend Omar and how he no longer was coming to school.

Then I thought of Omar's dad, who was now dead and being blamed for the bombing in the Pipes.

"Hold on," I told Tim, taking a step towards the two boys.

"Not on my watch, you don't," Tim growled.

I turned to face him. "They won't hurt me. I just want to talk to them." I stepped around Tim's large form.

Weston took a small step towards me, then quickly looked down at his feet before he spoke. "I wanted to say..." That's as far as he got before he fell silent and shuffled his feet. After a moment he started again. "I'm sorry about what happened in the Pipes."

I was so shocked by his words; it took me a moment to realize Manny was also telling me how sorry he was. When both boys turned to leave, I was able to finally speak up through my shock.

"I don't believe Gunny did it!" I said, and both Weston and Manny stopped. They turned and gave me questioning glances before Weston took a small step back to me.

"You don't?" he said with disbelief on his face.

"No, I don't. Gunny didn't hurt me when he kidnapped me," I explained, unsure why I was saying all of this but knowing I had to speak my mind, even if it wouldn't help Omar return to school. "He didn't hurt me and wouldn't have. He just wanted to explain things."

"What things?" Weston asked.

"Um." I didn't want to say too much. Weston and Manny weren't my friends, but I did want to make them understand I didn't blame Omar's dad for the bombing of my home hub. "He wanted to apologize for hurting me. He said he was sorry." At least that much was true.

"Oh." Manny gave me a nod, then his eyes moved past me to where Tim stood. "Well, ok."

"Thanks," I said quickly. When Weston looked confused, I continued. "For telling me you're sorry."

Both boys nodded and turned to enter the kitchen hall as I stood there thinking. Omar would never get to return to the Academy because of his father's actions. But it really wasn't Gunny's fault. It was Master Commander Joan Deller's fault.

After a moment I turned and followed Tim into the hall. I had just spotted a short line for one of the food tables when the noise in the hall died away, and I looked around. I saw two professors talking together, one with a tablet in her hands. Three students came rushing up to me.

"Is it true?" a girl from my accounting class asked me just as the noise from the room exploded.

"What?" I asked as several more students came forward and surrounded me.

"This is unbelievable!" a boy from my base class said as he shook my hand.

"When did you find out?" a student I had never seen before shouted at me just as Evan came over and pulled me from the center of the crowd.

"Evan, what is going on?" I demanded as several students followed us towards the doorway.

"Don't say anything!" Evan demanded as Tim came over and all but picked me up and carried me out of the hall.

When we reached the front of our dorm room, I was shocked to see several reporters out front. Tim still had his massive arm around me, and Evan had a firm hand on my other arm. I didn't know where Miles and Rafe were, but I was too distracted by the flashing of cameras and the reporters' shouted questions to think about it.

"When did you discover your heritage?" one shouted as

another demanded to know where I was going to live when school let out.

Tim shoved a path through the reporters and when we were finally in the building, he closed and locked the door behind us.

"Quickly, up to your room," Tim growled as he tried to block the entrance to ensure no one pushed their way past the closed door.

"Up here," Evan said and dragged me up the stairs.

When we entered our dorm room, I was relieved to see Rafe and Miles were already there. Miles was patting Rafe's shoulder as I entered and stopped. The two looked at me, and Rafe leapt forward and gave me a strong hug.

"What in the heck is going on?" I demanded. I was so confused. Maybe something had happened to Mia?

"Zane," Miles said, but he stopped when Rafe pulled away and looked at me. His dark eyes filled with tears as a smile formed on his lips.

"It's in the news. We're brothers!" Rafe said. He drew me in for a hug.

The exclusive news breakthrough came from an anonymous source. It told of how Hudson Adamson had taken a lover seventeen years before, one who lived in the Pipes. He had shamefully kept this lover for over a year until she became pregnant. Then, due to his high rank, he discarded the woman. She had died during the birth of her son, Zane.

The article spoke of Hudson's shame in having a Piper for a son and how he refused to acknowledge his relationship or have any involvement with the child. The article spoke of Zane and his grandmother living in squalor for years until his biological grandfather, Adam Waltson, paid for Zane's level schooling.

"Controller Adam Waltson was unavailable for comment; however, a source has confirmed that the Academy received a large donation to take in the delinquent boy called Zane Noman," the article went on to explain.

I grew so angry with the rest of the report that I wanted to toss the tablet across the room. However, since it was Evan's tablet, I lowered it to the bed and turned to look at Rafe, my brother.

"I don't have to ask you if you knew," Rafe said with a laugh.

"You're ok with this?" I asked in shock.

"Okay?" Rafe said with a laugh. "Heck, yeah! I always wanted a brother. Don't get me wrong, I love my little sister, but man! A brother!"

"But?" I stammered as Rafe pumped a fist in the air, then slowly turned to look at me.

"Z, my mom and dad were separated and divorced long before you were conceived. Mom remarried before I was two," Rafe said, reminding me he was that much older than me.

"The news makes it sound like your mom stole Hudson from his family," Miles said from across the room with a frown. "They don't paint a pretty picture of you, either, calling you a delinquent and saying you're always in trouble at school. They even hint that your mom died from shame."

"I'm sure Grandpa will get them to retract that." Rafe laughed. "Heck, Grandpa! He's your grandpa too!"

I didn't get the rest I needed that night and, before I knew it, I was expected to wake and take my last two tests for the year.

I had talked to Mia briefly about the article. She reassured me she was coming to my level ceremony and said we would talk then. I asked if she knew Hudson had been my father and she assured me she hadn't.

"Adalynn had many secrets, and your father was one of them," Mia explained.

The press had been escorted off campus, and I was grateful to be able to walk to my tests without being hounded by them. However, fellow students wanted to know all about my family. Some wanted to know how it felt to be rich. I was confused until they explained that Hudson had been a very wealthy man.

"I don't care about that," I said, reminding them I had my Z-rider company.

"Yeah, but that's nothing compared to Hudson's wealth," the boy tried to explain.

Somehow, I got through that day, though I wasn't even sure I'd finished the two tests. We ate in the kitchen hall that night and, to my shock, Rafe introduced me to everyone as his little brother.

That stumped a lot of our fellow students, as the news was reporting that Rafe's family was attempting to discredit the story that I was Hudson's child.

"What does your mother think?" I asked him after Evan had set his second plate of dessert on the table.

"Mom?" Rafe said as he snatched one of Evan's cookie orbs for himself. "She said she wasn't shocked. She said you look just like me two years ago."

"I do?" I grabbed a shiny plate and tried to get a good look at myself in its reflection.

I remembered what Rafe had looked like a year ago, but when I glanced in my reflection, I didn't see Rafe's strong chin. We both had dark hair and bushy eyebrows, but his nose had a stronger line, and his lips were rounder than mine. Plus, his eyes were brown whereas mine were an odd hazel.

"Yeah, except you have Dad's eyes. I have mom's brown ones." Rafe said with a shrug.

The day before the level ceremony, the news submitted a small retraction. The article said the reporter talked to a source from the school who stated that I was in fact a model student and had never caused any trouble while at the Academy. It also went on to explain that Rafe's family was ecstatic to discover our relationship and that I would be spending some time over the holiday with my grandfather and half-brother.

"I will?" I asked as I read it while sitting in my dorm.

"Of course, you will!" Rafe said with a smile. "I already made plans to show you all of my home. Of course, we have to work out the schedule with your grandmother. But Grandpa has written me twice about having you stay with him over the break."

"He did?" I asked. I opened my email to look for anything from Waltson. Sure enough, I had two messages from Adam.

"Zane, I wanted to tell you last year that you were my grandson, but I had made a promise to your mother before you were born. Adalynn was worried about you and wanted to raise you in the Pipes. She made Hudson and I promise not to interfere in your life until you are older. Her death didn't change her wishes, and so your father and I kept our distance while your wonderful grandmother raised you.

Now that the news has broken the story of our relationship, I wonder if you would like to join me on this break for a few days. I hope to get to know you better.

· · ·

Your grandfather, Adam."

There was another message similar to the first, giving the days and times that Adam would be available. I quickly forwarded them to Mia and asked if I could join Adam for those dates. Then I tuned back into the conversation around me.

"We have two new employees at the workshop. My dad's apprentice is actually staying there," Evan said with a smile. "Even with the recent news, our sales haven't dipped."

"Eventually we will run out of buyers," Miles said with a yawn.

"Not if we keep spitting out new models," Evan replied with a grin.

"Are your parents coming to the ceremony tomorrow?" Miles asked.

"Yeah," Evan replied. He looked over to Rafe and asked. "Are your mom and sister coming?"

"Yes, and our grandfather too," Rafe said with a grin aimed at me.

It was weird for me. I had been raised with only Mia as close family. But when the ceremony started, I suddenly found myself surrounded by not only Mia and Brad, but my brother Rafe, his mother Hadley, her husband Travis, and Rafe's little sister Aliyah. When Adam Waltson joined us before the service, I wanted to shout out all my secrets to him.

But Rafe had warned me to remain quiet that day. *"There will be plenty of time to tell Grandpa about Joan. Don't spoil our level ceremony by speaking about that woman."*

Evan and Miles were quick to concur. Outvoted, I agreed to keep these things to myself for now.

I was given a very warm welcome by Rafe's family, and Adam told me how proud he was of me. I was finally able to thank him for being my sponsor and paying for my education.

"I knew when I spoke to you that first time that you were a boy destined to go far," Adam said with a firm nod of his head. "And I was right. Your Zriders are amazing."

"You know about them?" I asked, feeling a little embarrassed.

"Know about them?" he said with a laugh. "I own four. Of course, three have the special handles. I almost broke my neck on the first one," he said with a wink.

The ceremony was as long as the one the previous year. Head Dean once again was in his element as everyone focused on him. He droned on about structure and explained how proud he was of each of the students. He made it sound as if the students relied on him to pass, but I wasn't listening much. My only concern now was my final grades. As I was finally called forward to receive my level two pin and paper, I took a deep breath. Once again, Mathew Carlson stepped forward and personally handed me my level two papers.

"Zane, I must say, this year's grades were outstanding," he said as he shook my hand.

My head buzzed all the way back to my seat. Until I opened the letter, I was still worried the grades were lower than the previous year's. To my amazement, I received higher marks in every class, including the difficult programing class.

When the ceremony was concluded, and the families of the students started for home, my friends gathered once again on the steps of our dorm. Breanna had snuck away to join us, and even Mitch was there for the first time. Our guards, Ryan and Tim, were a few feet away while we all sat around and talked.

"Well, another level completed," Evan said as he played with the shiny tan triangle on his school uniform.

"I'm just glad I passed accounting," Breanna said with a sigh. "Math and I don't get along."

I smiled and bumped her shoulder as she sat next to me. "I could always tutor you in math," I said, and Mitch laughed.

"You? The only reason you passed was because of my assistance," Mitch teased.

"Will you be able to come and visit us now?" Breanna asked as she looked up at me.

"Well, with Mitch staying there, and my newfound last name..." I said as I studied the level paper in my hand, which read Zane Hudson. "I'm guessing your mother might relent and let me visit you."

"If she doesn't, then we'll have you over," Rafe said with a wink as we all laughed.

As we sat there on the steps of the dorm room, I somehow knew this school break was going to be filled with fun and my newfound family.

It dawned on me that a new adventure was just around the corner. Suddenly, I had no restrictions, a new family, and endless possibilities.

Epilogue

Forcers' Master Commander Joan Deller was furious. She stood in her high office with her small hands balled around the paper as she stared off into space.

Her last plan had failed, and someone would pay for it. She had thought that leaking Zane's parentage to the press would cause Adam huge problems. Maybe even drop his popularity with the Prime Committee a few notches. Instead, Adam had demanded a retraction and the news had relented. Even the committee had voiced their displeasure at the press's harsh words regarding Adam's fool of a son.

She stood there in her high office and smiled; glad Hudson was dead. He had been a pain and an inconvenience to her. He had almost ruined everything a year ago, but his death had solved much for her.

Except....

A frown crossed her pretty face as she thought of Adam Waltson.

"The fool!" she hissed and once again crumpled the paper in her hands.

She would need to focus on the old man instead of trying to track down the witness who had seen her kill Hudson. After all, nothing had been revealed for over a year regarding this so-called witness.

She had tried to locate the person who might have seen her kill Hudson. She had even tried to discover if the Zane boy had been there. But no one was talking. Zane had outmaneuvered her in the Fixer hub several months before when she had grown impatient and shot her blast gun at him, hoping he would be too scared to return to school. But he had vanished that night, and her plans to run him out of the Academy had failed.

She sneered when she thought about Gunner Brackson and Simon Woodson. They both had been willing fools until Gunner had discovered her plans to kill the cripple. Then she'd had to kill Simon. Gunner had run and hid from her for months.

A smile formed on her lips when she thought of how smart she had been to blame Simon's death on Gunner. Blaming Gunner had been pure genius.

Yet, Gunner had remained hidden from her until just recently. At that time, she had taken matters into her own hands. But another frown formed on her face when she thought about her failed attempts to eliminate the crippled boy, Mitch. She didn't think about the innocent people who had died in her bombs, including the children she had killed. She only thought about Mitch escaping death.

"I'll get him eventually," she hissed. She turned back to glance down at the paper she held, and her mind turned to Adam once again as she read the words on the page.

"Cease all harmful actions towards Zane Hudson or your secrets will be exposed."

Joan Deller let out a primal scream as she tossed the paper across the room and smashed her hands against the thick glass wall of her office. Hate and anger filled her as she looked down at the city far below. She vowed that she would not let an old man dictate her actions.

When the plan came to her, her frown slowly turned to a smile, and the laugh she emitted bounced around her large office.

This new plan could solve all her problems and might result in her finally gaining the control she deserved.

Books by J.J. Anders

Genoa Chronicles

The Scholar

The Warrior

The Queen

The Fallen

The Hidden

The Gifted

The Exiled

The Betrayed

The Lost

Level Up

The Pipes

The Fixers

The Printers

About the Author

JJ Anders powerful imagination and love of writing has spawned the thrilling new world and enchanting characters of Genoa. As a furious reader and devoted mother, her passion for storytelling reaches full bloom to bring her magical stories to life for the enjoyment of readers everywhere of all ages.

Her fantasy series will leave you begging for more.